Borderlore

Borderlore

Folktales and Legends of South Texas

David Bowles

LAMAR UNIVERSITY press

ISBN: 978-1-942956-01-3
Library of Congress Control Number: 978-1-942956-01-3

Illustrated by José Melendez
Manufactured in the United States

Lamar University Press
Beaumont, Texas

For my tíos and tías

Linda Casas, Daniel Garza,
Michael Garza, Marie Shirley
and their spouses

for all the cuentos

Other books from Lamar University Press Include

Jean Andrews, *High Tides, Low Tides: the Story of Leroy Colombo*
Charles Behlen, *Failing Heaven*
Alan Berecka, *With Our Baggage*
David Bowles, *Border Lore, Folktales and Legends of South Texas*
David Bowles, *Flower, Song, Dance: Aztec and Mayan Poetry*
Jerry Bradley, *Crownfeathers and Effigies*
Kevin Casey, *Four-Peace*
Julie Chappell and Marilyn Robitaille, editors, *Writing Texas, 2013-14*
Terry Dalrymple, *Love Stories, Sort Of*
Robert Murray Davis, *Levels of Incompetence: An Academic Life*
William Virgil Davis, *The Bones Poems*
Jeffrey Delotto, *Voices Writ in Sand*
Gerald Duff, *Memphis Mojo*
Ted L. Estess, *Fishing Spirit Lake*
Mimi Ferebee, *Wildfires and Atmospheric Memories*
Ken Hada, *Margaritas and Redfish*
Michelle Hartman, *Disenchanted and Disgruntled*
Michelle Hartman, *Irony and Irreverence*
Katherine Hoerth, *Goddess Wears Cowboy Boots*
Lynn Hoggard, *Motherland, Stories and Poems from Louisiana*
Dominique Inge, *A Garden on the Brazos*
Gretchen Johnson, *The Joy of Deception*
Gretchen Johnson, *A Trip Through Downer, Minnesota*
Christopher Linforth, *When You Find Us We Will Be Gone*
Tom Mack and Andrew Geyer, editors, *A Shared Voice*
Dave Oliphant, *The Pilgrimage, Selected Poems: 1962-2012*
Janet McCann, *The Crone at the Casino*
Erin Murphy, *Ancilla*
Harold Raley, *Louisiana Rogue*
Carol Coffee Reposa, *Underground Musicians*
Carol Smallwood, *Water, Earth, Air, Fire, and Picket Fences*
Jim Sanderson, *Sanderson's Fiction Writing Manual*
Jim Sanderson, *Trashy Behavior*
Jan Seale, *Appearances*
Jan Seale, *The Parkinson Poems*
W.K. Stratton, *Ranchero Ford/Dying in Red Dirt Country*
Melvin Sterne, *The Number You Have Reached*
Robert Wexelblatt, *The Artist Wears Rough Clothing*
Jonas Zdanys, editor, *Pushing the Envelope: Epistolary Poems*

For more information go to
www.LamarUniversityPress.Org

Acknowledgments

It is important to note that any modern folklorist in the Rio Grande Valley necessarily stands on the shoulders of giants. I am forever indebted to the work of individuals like Adina De Zavala, Jovita González, J. Frank Dobie, Américo Paredes, Juan Sauvageau and José Limón, all of whom inspired me to dig deeper into the tales I'd heard as a child from my grandmother, Marie Garza, and all those tíos and tías who inherited her storytelling gift. The tutelage of Dr. Mark Glazer at Pan American University then led me to dismantle, examine, and rebuild those legends in ways that spoke to me as a native of the Valley in the 21st century. His approval of the present volume is greater affirmation than I could have ever hoped to have.

Several of these pieces appeared in somewhat different versions in the *Creature Feature* mini-series I wrote for *The Monitor* and in *Mexican Bestiary*.

Other Books by David Bowles

As author
The Smoking Mirror
Strange Texas Tales That Never Die, Volumes 1-4
Shattering and Bricolage
Creature Feature: 13 Frightening Folktales of the Río Grande Valley
Flower, Song, Dance: Aztec and Mayan Poetry
Mexican Bestiary
The Seed: Stories from the River's Edge

As editor
Along the River: An Anthology of Voices from the Río Grande Valley
Along the River 2: More Voices from the Río Grande
Along the River III: Dark Voices from the Río Grande
Donna Hooks Fletcher: Life and Writings
Stories That Must Not Die (2012-2013)—series editor

CONTENTS

Introduction

The Lower Rio Grande Valley of Texas—the Valley, as it is known by its inhabitants—includes the four Texas counties in the extreme south eastern part of the state. Three of these counties are along the Rio Grande River, the U.S. Mexican border. They are, from west to east, Starr, Hidalgo, and Cameron counties. The fourth, Willacy, is to the north of Hidalgo and Cameron counties. The communities of the area form a metropolitan area that includes the cities of Brownsville, Edinburg, Mission, Pharr, Weslaco, and McAllen (which is the most dynamic of these cities). The Rio Grande Valley is an area where over 80% of the population is Mexican-American. This is the poorest urban area in the country and has an unemployment rate of about 20 percent. At the same time, this is one of the fastest growing areas of Texas. Predominantly Mexican-American in culture, people in the region find it important to tell both traditional lore and more contemporary stories. Folklore and, specially, folk tales offer an excellent opportunity to understand the rich culture of the Valley.

The most common type of oral folklore today is the legend. These are stories that seem to be true but are almost always fictional. Dr. Bowles' book is a collection of legends that introduce readers to a contemporary view of the status of legends in the lower Rio Grande Valley today.

In spite of strong external pressures, the Mexican-American heritage of the Valley has continued in our time with great vibrancy. However, the folklore of this area has not been published sufficiently. There are many topics of major popular and scholarly interest in this culture; these include folktales, folk medicine and "curanderismo" (faith healing) about which many more publications are needed. *Border Lore* is a major contribution in the dissemination of the heritage of the area. Legends can tell us much about cultural values anywhere, and in our area legends are especially important because the Chicanos of the borderlands firmly believe that repeating their stories is important.

This book gives us an outstanding overview of the stories that in their various incarnations have survived into our rapidly changing world. Furthermore, as these stories are transmitted from generation to generation, Mexican Americans have updated their traditional tales to fit contemporary needs. This collection represents the best of both the traditional and the modern in oral narrative and Mexican American legends, and it does so through the inherent power of story telling.

The collection includes examples from many variations of legends such as "The Vanishing Hitchhiker" and "The Devil at the Dance." The book offers an excellent representation of both older, more traditional legends and contemporary legends. The materials are representative of the contemporary Mexican-American tale as a whole. These legends, both traditional and modern, are among the most common narrative genres of the Mexican-American community. The major interest in any collection of stories should be the inherent quality of its narratives. This anthology is a collection of tales told well. *Border Lore* represents the best in both traditional and contemporary story telling.

The Mexican-American community today is the largest minority group in the United States, and it will continue to grow for some time to come. This reality has created a growing interest in every aspect of Chicano culture in American life. *Border Lore* is an important contribution to publicizing this vibrant and expanding part of American culture.

Mark Glazer
Professor Emeritus
University of Texas-Pan American

Author's Preface

If folklore is the set of all cultural constructs—beliefs, customs, narratives, songs—passed mind to mind by a community down the years, then folktales are one of the most infectious vectors for spreading that culture. My own identity depended during formative years upon this transmission: as a boy and young man growing up in deep South Texas, I thrilled to the words of the storytellers around me, even as these memes were burrowing in my brain and shaping me. I can still hear the voices of my *tío* Joe on the ranch, my *tías* in their kitchens, my mom and dad at the dining table—but most especially I remember my grandmother, Marie Garza, sitting in a rocking chair while Los Panchos crooned softly on her record player and I listened spellbound with my brothers and cousins to the tale she wove with words and gestures.

And, ah, what wonders she let us see! Though her tales ranged from humorous to terrifying, I was most drawn to the horrors she described: weeping revenants, disembodied hands, shape-shifting witches, shadowy boogeymen. To this day I get a chill when I hear their names in Spanish—*llorona, mano pachona, lechuza, cucuy*. Yet what I feel is not fear, but a sort of thankful nostalgia, for the lessons I learned from those eerie narratives helped me make it through the darkest times of my life.

At school I heard variations on those same motifs from teachers and friends. Though I noted the differences in the particulars of each version, their recitation sparked a recognition of shared identity. As I grew older, I received new narratives, some the kind of hoary old folktales favored by the *ancianos,* but others of a more contemporary nature, legends that helped me find membership within broader communities like Generation X and the tech-savvy early adopters of the Internet.

The late folklorist Linda Dégh emphasized this communal identity function of legends for people within a particular folk group. Interestingly, however, she did not focus as have many others on the underlying structural elements of folktales and legends. While valuing the work of scholars like Propp, Aarne and Thompson, Dégh was more intrigued by the unique formulations of traditional narratives that arise from the rich and unpredictable intersection of circumstance and the storyteller's personality.

Likewise, while I am partly driven by a desire to preserve certain stories dear to my heart, my retellings result from my need to retransmit those narratives from my present space in life, embedding them in new contexts meaningful to me and to my prospective audience. Of course, this *contextualization* is a normal part of the transmission process: every time a folktale or legend is retold, the storyteller has to situate the timeless tale in a context the hearer will receive. Each retelling is a performance, as Gillian Bennett affirms, and the resources of a given storyteller influence the structure and trappings of the tale.

As a writer of fiction and poetry, my sensibilities and skills are more literary, so it is unsurprising that my contextualization of my favorite *cuentos y leyendas* would take the form of short stories. Folklorists like Daniel Barnes and Suzanne Ferguson have long noted the modernity of the contemporary or urban legend and its similarity to the short story in its elliptical plot structure, ratcheting up suspense before the climax and unravelling. That stylistic intersection fascinates me, and readers will note my tendency in the pages that follow to rework even the oldest of folktales into such a framework.

I began to retell my grandmother's stories in literary form twenty years ago. It was my second year as a teacher of middle-school English (and my first as a part-time lecturer at the university)—I had a horribly difficult class just after lunch, full of students who struggled to read and hated the state-adopted textbook. After an epiphany of sorts, I began using the folktales that they had heard, just like I had, at the knees of *abuelos* and *tíos*.

My very first written, literary performance was an early version of "Damnation at Toluca Ranch," contained in this volume. As I sat in my rolling chair in front of those twenty-five teenagers and read the story aloud, something changed. Where there had been conflict and misunderstanding, there was a shared identity. I had proven myself part of a group that included them, no longer just the teacher, but the storyteller, the mantle slipping from my grandmother's shoulders to drape across my own.

The respect I earned that day was humbling. I had come before young members of my community and shared something "with the stamp of good authority," to use Thompson's phrase, passed down to me by a wise woman who preserved our border lore.

I was hooked.

To this day, after I finish reading to them, kids ask me, "But is it *true*?" What a tough question! I always struggle to find an answer that slips between the false divisions we impose upon the world. Teenagers specifically have a hard time opening hearts and mind. Younger children do that best. Still, the problem of *truthfulness* remains.

Gillian Bennett has suggested that these stories can be told in essentially two ways (with a sort of graded continuum between them): *for laughs,* fast and sketchily, with a complicit understanding with the listener that no one actually believes this stuff; or *as true*, with great specificity about setting and character, orienting information, slowing of the plot for elaboration, deliberateness and care, energy and conviction.

For me there is no choice: I must work to retell these legends and folktales *as true*. Though I do not believe they describe *real* historical happenings, I most definitely believe that they are *true*. They speak truths that cannot be otherwise easily expressed about who we are and what matters to us, truths best seen juxtaposed against that darkness awaits—the old folks whisper down the centuries—just outside the door...

The Lady in Black

For decades, motorists traveling north along US Highway 281 have reported seeing a troubled woman wearing a black dress wandering near the intersection with FM 141, just south of Alice. When the travelers stop to help her, the sad figure vanishes into thin air, leaving them wondering who the phantom was and how she came to haunt this stretch of road.

The old folks, of course, know the tale.

In 1748, Colonel José de Escandón y Helguera—after two decades of suppressing indigenous revolts in the northern extremes of New Spain—was finally permitted to implement his plan to colonize the region between the Pánuco River and the Nueces: all of present-day Tamaulipas and south Texas. Escandón christened the colony Nuevo Santander, after the city in his native Cantabria, Spain. The Spanish crown named the colonel governor of the region and bestowed upon him the title *Count of Sierra Gorda*.

In addition to the many towns he himself established (Reynosa, Camargo, Mier), Escandón allowed other settlements to be set up by Tomás Sánchez de la Barrera y Garza, most famously the city of Laredo. Captain Sánchez was also tasked with taking a group of settlers to the northernmost edge of Nuevo Santander. After searching for a suitable site near the Nueces River, he finally guided the families to the fertile banks of Peñitas Creek, some twenty miles north of modern Alice. Sánchez oversaw the construction of a large house formed with white caliche blocks referred to as *Casa Blanca*, a name that would come to designate the whole settlement.

Legend has it that among the men and women who accompanied Sánchez on this venture was Don Raúl Ramos y Zúñiga and his young wife Leonora Rodríguez de Ramos. Occupying Casa Blanca after the departure of Captain Sánchez, the couple was soon managing a vast ranch teeming with *Retinto* cattle and Basque *vaqueros* imported from Spain. Don Raúl, a *peninsular* whose family was respected in the motherland, wielded great influence over the settlement. Nearly everyone admired him.

One ranch hand, however, found himself smitten the moment he laid eyes on Leonora: Lope Ibarra, whose fathers had served the family for generations. His blood curdled in his veins to see such beauty wasted on his *patrón*, whom he considered cold and obnoxious.

Why should he have everything? Ibarra fumed. Wealth, cattle, land, position—these he gets from his family. I understand: my family has none of these, so I likewise receive nothing. But Leonora...her loveliness should be earned by depth of feeling, not bartered in exchange for a name.

But there was nothing Ibarra could do, so he simply burned within, watching his beloved from afar, almost trembling with passion when his work brought him closer to her.

The couple had been at Casa Blanca for less than a year when pressing family business necessitated Don Raúl's immediate return to Spain. Leonora wanted to accompany him, but he would hear nothing of it.

"The trip is difficult, perilous. I saw several women succumb to illness and exposure on my voyage to this land, what seems ages ago. I will not risk your health just to rush across the sea and then return with equal haste. Besides, I need you to administer the ranch—the foreman is a good fellow, but these are not his lands."

Leonora might have pressed further, but there was a glint in her husband's eyes that dissuaded her. Though normally genteel and calm, Raúl had a reputation for extreme mood swings, explosions of violence and vitriol that she hoped she would never see. Better to heed his wishes and pray the time would fly.

During the six months her husband was away, Leonora discovered with great joy that she was pregnant. But her giddiness was soon soured by the unwanted attentions of Lope Ibarra, who first discreetly and then with increasing boldness attempted to woo her, speaking badly of his *patrón* in hopes of winning her heart.

Leonora, of course, rebuffed his every advance, and Ibarra swore revenge.

With lavish gifts–a string of pearls, a sumptuous black dress from Paris–Don Raúl returned, glad to be reunited with his lovely wife and ecstatic at the news that he would soon be a father. When he set out riding across his ample ranch, however, he was approached by Ibarra, who with great remorse revealed a horrible secret: Leonora had been unfaithful to her husband, repeatedly. The child she carried was not his.

Raúl, who had trusted three generations of Ibarras, flew into an incontrollable rage at the news. Trembling, blind with fury, he spat an ominous command:

"Take another man, one who can keep his tongue still, and seize her. Ride south with her for two hours, then find a sturdy mesquite tree and hang the traitorous wench. Leave her body twisting in the wind!"

Ibarra nodded and rushed to comply, a sneer of wicked delight on his devilish lips. With the aid of his best friend, he dragged Leonora screaming from Casa Blanca, bound and gagged her, and galloped off into the chaparral.

Upon his return, he found Don Raúl drinking, his hands still shaking, his eyes hollow with despair and hatred.

"It's done, *patrón*."

Raúl said nothing. He did not even acknowledge Ibarra's presence.

For three days, the aristocrat subsumed himself in a drunken stupor. On the morning of the fourth, he road to where his wife's body had been abandoned. Overcome by regret, he wept to see his beloved Leonora, ravaged by wind and sun and predator, still wearing her new and costly dress. Taking his wife down gently, he buried her and the unborn child beneath the mesquite tree.

Madness crept slowly into his mind, month after month, year after year. He swore he could see her spirit when he explored the southernmost edges of the ranch. She was always wearing the black gown, beseeching him with a raised hand.

The time came that he could bear the haunting and the guilt no more. He took up a flint lock pistol and put a lead ball in his brain.

To this day, the people of Jim Wells County swear that Leonora's spirit roams the lonely spaces near the place of her murder. She is looking for Raúl, some say, hoping to finally prove that she remained faithful to him until the very end and well beyond, that the child she carried was truly his.

She will never find him, of course. His own hand damned his wretched soul.

The Big Bird

For two months in early 1976, the Rio Grande Valley was plagued by a massive flying beast known only as the Big Bird. On the evening of January 7, San Benito policemen Arturo Padilla and Homero Galván separately spotted a strange winged form as they patrolled. That same night, Alvérico Guajardo caught sight of the same creature in Brownsville: he described it as a giant bat. A week later an airborne monster with leathery skin and simian features attacked Armando Grimaldo of Raymondville.

After that incident, there came an avalanche of reports. A group of teachers driving to San Antonio witnessed what they swore was a prehistoric pteranodon. National media picked up the story. Johnny Carson joked about the Big Bird on *The Tonight Show*. But when a reward was offered, hoaxes started cropping up. Finally, the news reported the capture of a *jabiru*, an enormous South-American stork, and broadcast video of a large blue heron native to Texas. Many people believed the mystery of the Big Bird solved, and the media turned to other stories. But those who had encountered the creature, including the Perales family, insist to this day that it still haunts the skies of south Texas.

In the intense cold of a pre-dawn January morning, Manuel Perales pulled his beaten truck onto a deer lease in northern Hidalgo county. His son Danny sat in sullen, sleepy silence as Perales hopped out of the cab and began pulling supplies from the rust-eaten bed.

"*Ándale, m'ijo,*" he called. "Grab your rifle and help me get the cooler to the deer stand. *Vamos.*"

Danny said nothing, but he yanked the Remington off the gun rack and exited. The ground was a little frozen and crunched under his boots. Making his way around the truck, he slung the .30-06 over his shoulder and sighed. He had no desire to be out in the cold, especially not to hunt deer.

He had been taught to shoot since he was very young, his father training him first with an air gun and then a .22 till he was, like all Perales men, a crack shot. Since turning twelve a few months ago, however, he had realized he didn't want to kill animals. He'd shot a squirrel from a tree at his uncle Jesse's house, but when he'd looked it in the eye there in the dust, that solid blue eye that seemed to beg for mercy, he had discovered that he was not a hunter. The coup de grace he gave the squirrel would be the last shot he'd ever take. He swore it.

His father wouldn't understand, of course, so he kept quiet. Grabbing one end of the ice chest that held their food, he followed his father to the wooden stand they'd rented. Built in the midst of a copse of mesquite, it gave them ample cover. They lugged the cooler up the ladder, ate their tacos in silence, and spread a San Marcos blanket out to lie upon as they awaited the huge buck that Manuel Perales affirmed with quiet surety they would bag.

The hours dragged by, cold and relentless. The sky lightened, but the clouds hung low and gunsteel gray. Danny had just begun to slip into a light sleep when a twig snapped below. He and his father both gripped their rifles tighter just as a magnificent 12-point stag stepped out of the brush fifty yards away.

Manuel motioned for his son to wait and, tensing up as he sighted along the barrel, the older man gently squeezed. Nothing happened. The rifle was jammed. Muttering a hoarse curse, he jerked his head at his son. *Your turn. Take the shot.*

His guts twisting with nausea, Danny looked through the scope, lining up the crosshairs with the buck's heart. Its head swiveled as if it had seen him. Dark liquid eyes peered up at the stand with primitive fear. Danny found that he couldn't do it. Couldn't pull the trigger. Couldn't kill that mighty king of the brush. The stag bolted and disappeared into the thick clumps of acacia, ebony and wild olive.

"Danny!" his father called. "What in the..."

His shout cut off abruptly as his body was yanked upward into the sky. Rolling over, Danny saw massive talons curled around his father's chest. Enormous wings beat at the winter air, lifting the man higher and higher in jerks. A whistling screech chittered in a crooked, serrated beak above which alien eyes glowed with phosphorescent fury. It was the Big Bird!

Danny didn't hesitate a second. Leaping to his feet, he lifted the Remington, and in a single, smooth motion ejected the cartridge, slid the bolt home to chamber a new round, aimed at a malicious eye and fired. The beast howled in pain and released his father, sending him tumbling through the air to thud painfully against the worn wood of the stand. The Big Bird, badly wounded, wheeled off into the distance upon its leathery wings.

Manuel suffered only cracked ribs, which healed with time. But he never forgot the courage of his son. And Danny learned that, while not a hunter, he could take the shot when it mattered.

He still watches the skies.

The Devil at Boccaccio 2000

The old folks tell us that, in his quest to tempt souls and lead them to perdition, the Devil visits dancehalls and discotheques all around the world. He was sighted in Danzig, Germany, in the late 1800s, dancing with a young girl who was saved when the band changed their waltz to a hymn. Not long afterward, in Quebec, Canada, young Rose Latulippe fell victim of Satan's fondness for dance.

In Mexico there have also been reports of the Devil's appearing at *bailes*—as when the Prince of Darkness nearly killed a girl in the 1930s in Matehuala, San Luis Potosí.

None of these sightings, however, can match his legendary visit to McAllen, Texas, on Good Friday of 1979.

Magdalena Mares had just turned sixteen, but her beauty had already attracted the admiration of more than one senior boy. Of course, her parents—strict Catholics—would never allow her to date. So, though the attention was flattering, she shyly rejected their advances, behavior her friends considered "totally bogus."

Yet as she labored away at home, prayed her rosary, attended mass, spent every waking moment in the company of her family, Magdalena realized that something was missing from her life. Fun. A sense of adventure. A touch of danger. She couldn't understand *why*, exactly, she felt the need for excitement and change, but there it was.

Then, the Monday of Holy Week, a gorgeous athlete named Jimmy Lucio approached her with an irresistible smile.

"You want to go with me to Boccaccio 2000 this Friday?"

Magdalena nearly fainted. The club was the trendiest, most happening hang-out in the Rio Grande Valley.

But she could imagine her parents' refusal. Go dancing? At a discotheque? Where they sell alcohol? On Friday the 13th? And a Good Friday at that? They were liable to lock her away until they could marry her off.

"I don't know, Jimmy," she muttered, embarrassed. "Yeah, I would love to go, but my parents..."

His smile dissolved as he nodded. "Okay, I dig." She started to explain, but he waved her words away. "It's alright, Magda. Maybe another time."

On the phone that evening, her friend Andrea assured her there would be no other time. "Are you crazy? Jimmy Lucio asks you to Boccaccio 2000 and you *turn him down*? Call him up. Tell him you'll meet him there. Then just lie to your parents and say you're eating dinner at my house. I'll lend you a fab dress, and you can go boogie with that hunk!"

It was a solid plan, and Magdalena found herself agreeing. Jimmy said he was fine with meeting up at the club, and Mr. and Mrs. Mares never suspected a thing.

The evening of April 13, 1979, Magdalena—looking amazing in Andrea's *quinceañera* gown—stepped into Boccaccio 2000. Lights strobed and spun, Donna Summer crooned "Bad Girls" over a driving disco beat, and a morass of bodies swirled across the dance floor. Magdalena navigated a sparkling dry ice haze, searching for Jimmy's dark curls and flashing eyes.

She spotted him at last, leaning over a pretty *güera* he'd backed against a wall. Furious, jealous and ashamed, Magdalena threw herself onto a stool in the darkest recesses of the club. *Coming here was a mistake*, she thought with a bitter pang. *I'll leave when this song is over.*

At that moment, the heavy metal doors swung open and a man strode in. Impeccably dressed and breathtakingly handsome, he slid his eyes across the writhing crowd, hunting for someone. Then his gaze fell on Magdalena, and her stomach was set ablaze. Her limbs trembling, she watched as with deliberate and patient steps he ambled toward her, the dancers parting as if by instinct to let him through.

In moments he stood before her, his orange-brown eyes glittering, a leering smile revealing small, predatory teeth. He said nothing, just stretched out his hand and inclined his sleek head. Magdalena found she could not resist. She closed her fingers round his and he pulled her to the center of the crowd. The Pointer Sisters began singing "Fire," and the couple spun across the dance floor like practiced partners.

As she twirled in the stranger's arms, the rest of the world receded. All that existed were those eyes, like dark suns preparing for supernova, and his voice, which whispered her name again and again in a lover's hushed tones.

She could not hear the screams, did not see hands raised to gaping mouths, fingers pointing in frantic staccato. She was already lost.

"His feet!" the scattering dancers cried, fleeing the acrid smell of sulfur that curled from the spinning couple. The DJ abandoned his turntables as he saw through the reddish haze that the stranger's legs ended in a goat hoof and rooster claw.

No one dared approach, though the demon's hands burned black prints upon the girl's exposed flesh every time he caressed her shoulders, back, arms. Her eyes rolled back into her head...she began to seize violently, foam specking her lips.

Abruptly, the song ended. The stranger let go of Magdalena, who slumped lifeless to the floor. He strode from the club without a word as the crowd looked on in impotent horror. A black car was waiting for him. He got in and disappeared into the night.

And Magdalena? An ambulance soon rushed her body away. Some say she died that night, cautioning young girls about sneaking out to indulge in sinful deeds.

But a few claim she still lives, her beauty slowly fading as she waits for that handsome stranger to return for her.

The Ghosts of Fort Brown

Not long after moving into her dorm at the Village at Fort Brown, Linda Flores was surprised to hear her roommate, Claudia Romero, dismiss the stories of ghosts with a laugh.

"That's just a bunch of nonsense, Linda. There's no such thing as ghosts. People just want to make university life sound cooler than it is."

"But, Claudia, think of all the thousands of people who died here: the Mexican-American War, the Civil War, the cholera epidemic—"

"So?" her friend shrugged. "People die all the time, every-where. Doesn't mean their spirits are haunting every square inch of the planet."

"No," Linda said, trying to be patient, "but here they dug up the bodies and moved them a hundred years ago. Or so they said. Then one summer three hurricanes hit one after the other, and they found coffins and stuff floating in the resaca. I'm pretty sure there are still bones under our feet, disturbed by our every step, restless."

But Claudia laughed all of this off until a few weeks later. Linda was awakened in the middle of the night by her roomie's startled gasp.

"Dude, that's not funny!" the skeptical freshman squeaked.

"What's not funny?"

"You yanked on my foot! Trying to make me think this room's haunted, huh? I've got a test tomorrow!"

"I swear I didn't do anything..."

"Ow! Hey, wait, how're you doing that if you're still in your bed?"

Linda sat up quickly, staring into the darkness on the other side of the dorm. A faint blue glow came from the near Claudia's feet. She leaned forward, squinted, and then she saw him. A little boy, crouching near the desk, dressed in old-fashioned clothes. His eyes were sunken and sad, and they fell on Linda with a spark of understanding. The boy stood and lifted his hand toward her. His pale lips moved, but there was no sound.

Leaping from her bed, Linda rushed to the light switch and flipped it up, flooding the room with illumination. But the boy was gone.

"What the heck are you doing?" Claudia demanded, clapping a hand over her eyes.

"I saw something. A little boy. A...A ghost."

"Whatever. Turn off the lights. I've had it with your stupid games. If I fail this test, I'm going to kick your butt."

After that night, Linda's life changed. Everywhere she walked on the UTB campus, she kept catching glimpses of specters out of the corner of her eye: soldiers standing in gloomy corners, women's faces floating in window panes, military nurses roaming at dusk. Having grown up in a very spiritual home with a *curandera* grandmother and aunts who dabbled in practical magic, Linda wasn't too frightened: she had the protection of the saints and the Virgin. But she was very concerned.

Most troubling was the figure of a lonely woman she kept seeing as she passed Gorgas Hall on her way to class every other day. Dressed in solemn black, the figure ambled back and forth, her eyes searching, her hands twisting in obvious worry. Linda, who knew that revenants haunt a place due to unfinished business, decided she simply had to help.

One Sunday afternoon, she went across the bridge into Matamoros to visit her grandmother, Doña Isabel. When Linda explained about the continued visits from the little boy, about the flitting specters, about the lady in black, the old curandera nodded sagely.

"I always hoped one of my grandchildren would have the Sight. And you have not panicked, which speaks highly of your faith and compassion. I would like to accompany you to your university. I am intrigued by some of the lost spirits who have attached themselves to you. There may be a reason."

Linda helped Doña Isabel gather the tools of her trade, and they drove back to Brownsville as the sun began to set. In the dorm room, they burned copal incense and Isabel murmured strange prayers, her gnarled fingers gracefully slipping over the beads of her rosary. Closing her eyes, the curandera reached out to the spiritual plane.

"He is here, but he hides. Lonely, afraid. All he sees is you, now. But he is longing for someone else." Sighing, Isabel stood and gestured toward the window. "Take me to the woman."

They trudged through the darkling dusk to Gorgas Hall, and Doña

Isabel clutched at Linda, doubling over. "Ah, this place...this is the old morgue. Here that *gringo* doctor tried to cure the sick. But he was like a child, William Gorgas, cutting open the dead, experimenting blind. Then he buried them without ceremony. Small wonder they haunt this place."

Linda glimpsed movement and pointed. "It's her, abuela. The woman."

Isabel pulled an amulet and sheaf of herbs from her bag. Mumbling soft incantations, she approached the revenant, whisking the air. The woman stopped her restless shuffling, her sunken eyes wide, her indigo halo brighter.

"I understand," whispered Isabel. "I know where he is. But you need a vehicle."

Linda stepped closer to her grandmother. "Abuelita?"

"She must attach herself to someone to travel to her son. The boy in your room. He died first, but she was too sick to ensure his proper burial. Now each searches for the other fruitlessly in the space death circumscribed for them."

Steeling herself, Linda nodded. "I'll do it. I'll take her to her son."

Within seconds, she felt icy fingers sink into her shoulders, a cold presence clamping against her spine. Driven by the mother's century-old grief, she rushed back to her room. The boy shot up from the cement floor, arms outstretched, running toward her.

With Linda as their conduit, mother and son embraced, their spirits freed in that instant to move beyond, together.

And Linda discovered in that instant her true calling: not just the nursing degree she had come to pursue, but the liberation of trapped souls. Let us wish her well.

Damnation at Toluca Ranch

Florencio Sáenz was an ambitious man who grew up admiring the wealthy landowners along the Río Grande. Gifted with a sharp mind for figures and languages, he eventually become bookkeeper for the Tampacuas Ranch, a sprawling spread carved out of the Llano Grande Land Grant in 1836, the year of Florencio's birth, by Don Antonio Cano.

After a decade of work, Florencio had done pretty well for himself. However, he wanted more, much more. As he surveyed the vast lands of his boss, which stretched from modern Nuevo Progreso to Edcouch, he dreamt of schemes to make his fortune.

One day, tiring of the daily drudge and yearning for a quicker way to attain his dreams, Florencio approached a shaman living on Agua Negra Ranch.

"Tell me...how can I become a rich landowner like Don Antonio?"

The *brujo* eyed him cautiously, his brow furrowed in thought. "I know someone who can help you," he said at last, "but I doubt you will approve."

Excited, Florencio rasped, "I'll do anything, talk to anyone."

"Very well. Every new moon, at midnight, when darkness is thick," the *brujo* whispered, "the Devil appears near a crumbling house on the banks of the river. If you go there, Señor Sáenz, he will give you what you desire."

Though Florencio was afraid, his fear waned as the date of the new moon approached. That night he got on his horse and rode to meet the Devil. He had seen the ruined house before, so he arrived without problems. As midnight approached, the dark air got colder, and beside the house appeared a handsome, well-dressed gentleman. Florencio knew in an instant that this was Satan himself.

"So, Don Felipe," said the Prince of Darkness, "you want easy wealth."

Florencio nodded, a little nervous but quivering with greed. "Yes."

"Excellent. I'll make you one of the wealthiest landowners along the Río Grande. You will be powerful, revered by many men. But I have two conditions." Here the Devil leaned in close and whispered in Florencio's ear. "At the end of your life, your soul will be mine. And you will never, ever, have a child."

Florencio gulped as the Devil smiled and stepped away.

"So, Florencio. Do we have a bargain?"

Though he was more frightened than ever, the bookkeeper agreed.

From that day, life changed for Florencio. Don Antonio confided in him more and more, regarding him as a better business partner than his own sons. The youngest Cano daughter, Sostenes, blossomed into womanhood, and Don Antonio permitted the much older Florencio to court her. Upon his deathbed, the old man gave his blessing for their marriage.

Sostenes inherited a large tract of land that the newlyweds dubbed Toluca Ranch. Florencio established a mercantile store, and soon he was widely respected for his level-headed business sense. By 1882 he had become an Hidalgo county commissioner, rubbing elbows with the powerful. But try as they might, the Sostenes could not seem to get pregnant. She was devastated.

Florencio was wracked by guilt, bitterly remembering his pact with the Dark One. So when tragedy left their niece Manuela an orphan, he agreed without hesitation to adopt her.

As the years passed and Manuela grew into a beautiful young woman, Florencio regretted the deal that he had made. Having found a loophole for one of the conditions, he searched for a way to snatch his soul from the Devil's grasp. Inspired by the digging of a well that produced bountiful sweet water, the landowner invited the local diocese to build a church on his ranch. The Church of St. Joseph the Worker was a lovely little building, and for many years Florencio sought divine intervention, salvation for his bartered spirit.

There was no slackening of his greed for wealth or power, sadly. He continued to buy up property, establish multiple businesses, serve the

Tejano political machine. When the Mexican Revolution erupted and the *sediciosos*, Texas Mexicans longing for independence, began attacking men they believed were complicit in keeping their people down, Florencio Sáenz was one of their targets. Even as the lively 79-year-old joined the cause of Texas Anglos, naming suspected rebels, Florencio found himself under attack.

His workers fled. The fields lay untended. The cattle began to die. By the end of 1915, Florencio was forced to shut down the ranch operations and move his family to Mercedes, where he spent the final decade of his life in relative anonymity and daily prayer.

In 1927, at the age of ninety-one, Florencio felt Death sidle close. He knew the end of his long, hard-bought life was upon him.

"Take me to the chapel," he told his son-in-law Amador. The family loaded his now frail form into a motorcar and drove him out to his beloved ranch, long fallen into disrepair. They carried him inside the church, settling him upon a cot near the altar. Looking up at the painted sailcloth ceiling, arching high like a vaulted cathedral, he pondered his life, unsure at the end whether his bargain had been worth his soul.

Florencio gripped his wife's hand as the light began to fade. His daughter's lips brushed his forehead. He heard distant sobs for a moment, and then his soul was free, drifting down the aisle and through the tall, narrow doors.

Outside waited, not the debonair gentlemen, but a mass of darkness in which roiled agonized forms—the sorrowful shapes of men and women Florencio's greed had destroyed.

Without a sound, a tendril emerged from the impossible black, coiling round his meager spirit. Stripped of all possessions and power, Florencio was dragged into the void.

The One-Eyed Woman

When Davey Garza emerged from Crockett Elementary that Friday afternoon in March of 1958, he was surprised to see his teenaged sister Marie waiting for him. Their house wasn't that far away, and he usually walked the couple of miles with a group of friends.

"Hey, ReRe," he called. It was a nickname the family used to differentiate between her and their mother, also named Marie. "What's up?"

"Mom and Dad wanted me to walk you home today, Davey. People are a little nervous right now, and even our parents don't want to take any chances."

"Nervous about what?" Davey asked as they began to amble down the sidewalk, his superstitious ten-year-old feet avoiding every crack.

"Well," ReRe said, "I guess it's the one-eyed woman that's got them all worked up."

A strange feeling of dread curled in the pit of Davey's stomach. "What are you talking about?"

"You mean the kids at school haven't said anything? Weird. Let's see...I guess it was a week ago that it started. Last Friday night, right outside Molina's Grocery Store."

"The competition," Davey intoned, sounding just like his father Manuel, owner and operator of the Handy Dandy, first convenience store in McAllen, Texas, to sport self-serve gas pumps.

ReRe went on. "So apparently an old woman was sitting on the bus stop bench. A younger lady came out of Molina's with a couple of bags of groceries in her arms, hurrying over to the bus stop to catch the next bus. She spotted the woman on the bench, looking away into the distance, and politely said hi. The old woman turned around, and the younger lady was shocked to see she had only one very large eye in the middle of her forehead. Screaming, she dropped her bags and ran back into the store.

When the manager came out there was no one sitting on the bench, and the poor scared lady's groceries were scattered all over the parking area."

The teenager stopped for a second to pull a burr from one of her bobby socks.

"But that's nothing, ReRe. She probably just had the sun in her eyes or something. There's no such thing as a one-eyed woman. Even in the *Odyssey* the Cyclops is a guy."

"Well, that wasn't the only sighting, Davey. Just yesterday, a taxi driver was looking for a fare in the area of Jasmine and North 23rd Street in McAllen when a woman suddenly darted out in front of his cab. There was no way of avoiding her. Even though he slammed the brakes hard, he still hit the old woman. She was thrown on top of the hood of his cab with her face close to his windshield. You can imagine his shock when he saw a face looking at him with only one big eye. He got out of his cab and tried to flag down oncoming cars for help. When someone finally stopped, the old woman he had hit was gone."

"Nah, I bet he made it up."

"They say the damage to his cab showed that he had definitely hit someone. But then, about thirty minutes after the report of this accident was received at the police station, a lady living in those apartments—what's the name...oh!—living in Retama Village heard a knock at her front door. She was home alone with a small baby and looked out the glass pane in her door before opening it up. Much to her surprise one large eye was looking back at her."

Davey shrugged. His big sister had inherited their mother's storytelling gift, and he had to admit she painted a pretty spooky picture in his mind, but he figured it was all a lot of silly gossip or attempts to make up a new scare to replace la Llorona in kids' minds. That's just what he told ReRe.

"Sure," she half-heartedly agreed as they walked up the driveway to their house. "And Mom and Dad don't actually think there's a monster wandering McAllen or anything. But they are concerned that maybe a crazy old woman might be trying to scare people, and they just asked me to keep you safe."

ReRe prepared dinner while Davey watched their little brother Danny, a three-year-old who couldn't keep his hands off of anything.

Friday was one of the busiest days of the week at the Handy Dandy, and their parents would be working until late. Davey had no problem with that, because it meant he could enjoy a two-and-a-half-hour block of all his favorite shows: *Saber of London*, *The Adventures of Jim Bowie*, *Zane Grey Theater*, *M Squad* and *The Thin Man*.

It was 9 pm when this marathon of Friday television ended. Danny had fallen asleep on the sofa beside him, so Davey stood carefully and quietly, stretching a little before walking to the window to check whether his parents were driving up the road.

His heart skipped a beat, and he jerked away in horror.

Standing on the sidewalk outside his house stood an old woman with a single eye in the middle of her forehead. She slowly lifted her arm and pointed at him.

"ReRe?" he managed to croak. "ReRe!"

He ran to his sister's room. She was lying on her bed, doing homework and talking on the telephone.

"ReRe!" he called, breathlessly. "There's...I mean, the one-eyed woman! She's in front of our house!"

ReRe shook her head and sighed. "Look, I'll call you back tomorrow. My brother is flipping his lid at the moment, sorry."

"Come *on!*" he squealed, grabbing her arm and tugging her along. When they reached the window, however, the strange figure was no longer there.

"Are you sure you saw her? Maybe it's from too much television. I mean, you yourself said the story was probably made up."

Davey swallowed hard. His mouth was dry with fear. "Yeah, but that was before I saw her with my own eyes! She looked at me, Sis! She...she *pointed* at me, like she wants to get me or something!"

"Okay, okay," she said, hugging him. "I believe you. But...maybe we shouldn't tell Mom and Dad about it. They're already under a lot of pressure. Don't want them to go ape on us, do you?"

"Okay, but you have to sleep with me and Danny tonight."

ReRe smiled. "Fine. And if she shows up again, we'll call the cops. I promise."

The night passed with no further strangeness, and after tossing and turning a good bit, Davey slept soundly till awakened to accompany the rest of the family to open the store. ReRe and her mother counted the money and got the register ready. Little Danny was allowed to play with his toys in the office while Davey helped his father stock the shelves and sweep the floor.

His last task was to wipe down the gas pumps, but as he shuffled through the doors, rag in hand, he was frozen in place, his whole body trembling.

It was the one-eyed woman again, standing in the middle of 23rd Street, pointing at him. She opened her mouth as if to speak, but Davey spun around and rushed back into the Handy Dandy.

"Dad!" he screamed. "It's the one-eyed woman! I saw her yesterday, too, but ReRe said not to tell you and now she followed me here and she's standing in the street like she wants to get me!"

"¿Qué cosa?" He turned to look at his daughter. "Is that true?"

ReRe started to reply, but Manuel Garza hurried outside. They could see him through the glass, looking this way and that. After a few seconds, the bell rang as he came back in.

"Nothing there, David."

"That's what happened last night, too," ReRe quickly explained. "He told me she was outside, but when I looked..."

Their father rubbed his hand across his face. "I need a smoke. You two should be helping, not making things difficult by joining in the crazy hysteria of...of...un montón de viejas chismosas." He stamped his way back to his office.

Marie Garza looked at first Davey and then ReRe. She sighed. "Children, your father doesn't need the added headache of your antics. And here I am, trying to get him to cut back on the tobacco..."

"Me lleva el demonio!"

The door to the office swung open. "Marie, your adorable son spilled my pouch out all over the floor and got milk in my pipe! And God knows what he did with my darn matchbox!"

Davey's mother rubbed her temples in exasperation. "ReRe, drive your brothers home and then come right back. Davey, you're going to watch Danny for a while, just until the morning rush is over."

"But, Mom, the one-eyed..."

"Son," she said warningly, "I love legends as much as anyone, but that is quite enough. Go wait in the car."

His shoulders slumped, Davey slouched across the parking lot to the sedan. He threw himself sullenly into the passenger seat and slammed the door. A few tears dribbled down his cheeks, but he wiped them away angrily.

Not going to let her see me cry, he thought. *Traitor. Made me look like I'm nuts or pranking.*

He reached up to twist the rear view mirror toward him, wanting to make sure his eyes weren't puffy and red. As he peered at his reflection, he saw sudden movement from the back seat.

His eyes widened in horror.

Behind him sat the one-eyed woman. Her gray hair was a mess of unruly curls, her skin brown and deeply wrinkled, her black dress lined with silvery lace.

The large single eye in the middle of her forehead stared unblinkingly at him, a dark purple iris nearly as black as the dilated pupil at its center.

She opened her thin, pale lips, revealing crooked yellow teeth.

"Do not scream." Her voice was unexpectedly sweet and kind. Its melody seemed to transfix Davey. He could not move. "Listen closely. Something very bad is going to happen today. I cannot quite see what, but I can see you, child. You are at the pivot of possible futures. You and only you can stop the tragedy. I see flames, death. Be alert. Do what must be done."

Then she opened the door and slipped out. By the time Davey turned around, she was gone.

"What are you looking for? There's nothing there, for crying out loud!"

It was ReRe, sliding Danny into the seat beside him and getting behind the wheel. Davey said nothing. He just sat quietly the whole way home, thinking of the woman's words.

Maybe she's been trying to warn people. They flip when she shows up, but that eye... Maybe it lets her see things we can't.

"The lady who dropped the bags," he said finally, just as the car pulled up to their house. "What ever happened to her?"

"Who? Oh. Yeah. A couple of days later she was in a nasty accident.

Still in the hospital. That's part of what has people all worked up, the way you're getting. They figure the old woman cursed her or something."

I knew it. Davey got out and Danny clambered after him, babbling softly as they walked up to the porch. ReRe unlocked the door and accompanied them inside.

"Are you going to be okay? It would be a bad idea to call up the store because you supposedly saw her again."

Davey shook his head. "No, I'm fine. I don't think she needs to show up anymore."

She sighed. "What a kookie brother you're turning out to be. Anyway, lock the door. I'll be back by lunch."

Davey did as she told him, then sat Danny on the couch to watch television as he slowly walked from room to room. *I am at the pivot, she said. I can stop the tragedy. But what's the danger? Where is it coming from?*

He stood in his sister's room for the longest time, his hand resting on the telephone, listening. Gradually, he noticed that mixed in with the laughing and applause from the television set was a tearful whimpering and a strange crackling hiss.

Bolting to the living room, Davey found his little brother surrounded by hungry flames. Clutched in the toddler's hand was their father's matchbox.

"Oh, no!" For a moment, panic seized at Davey, render-ing him motionless before the growing blaze. Then the words of the one-eyed woman echoed in his heart: "Do what must be done." He suddenly remembered his Boy Scout training. Fires must be smothered.

Dashing back to ReRe's bedroom, he ripped her comforter from the bed and ran to the living room. Dropping it on the flames that cut him off from his brother, Davey stamped solidly before snatching up Danny, unlocking the door with shaking hands, and bursting out into the morning sunlight.

Mr. Silva, their neighbor, was watering his lawn. When he saw the smoking spilling from inside, he hurried in with his hose. The fire hadn't spread too far, and within minutes it was completely out.

The Silvas called the Handy Dandy, and the boys' parents rushed home, throwing their arms about their sons in relief. They praised Davey for his bravery, calling him a hero. His family would never forget how he'd saved Danny's life and their home that day.

And Davey would forever remember the strange one-eyed woman who had ignored a young boy's fear in order to warn him. She was the true hero, he knew, though no one would ever believe him. Nameless and reviled, she had saved him all the same.

He prayed others elsewhere would heed her warnings.

The Devil's Lagoon

Many bodies of water in Texas are said to be haunted by ghosts of some sort, from wailing specters to silent revenants. One of the most famous of these locations is a small lake near San Perlita in Willacy County known informally as the *Devil's Lagoon.*

Growing up in the decade following World War II, Greg Montalvo heard the story at his grandmother's knee: in 1895, scant years after Richard King had wrangled a chunk of the San Juan de Carricitos land grant out of the hands of its rightful heirs, a young man and woman living on the King Ranch decided to get married. Their parents made arrangements for a ceremony at a chapel some hours distant, and on the auspicious day, a procession of wagons and carriages set out, transporting the wedding party.

Partway through the journey, the driver of the coach that contained the bride, the groom and their parents inexplicably pulled off the accustomed road, taking a shortcut that passed by means of a rickety wooden bridge over a deep lagoon. The passengers called out in alarm at the route, only to be ignored by the driver, who whipped the horses into a flat-out run. Halfway across, the bridge suddenly collapsed under their weight, plunging them into dark water that both pressed against the doors and poured in through the windows.

The bride and groom, realizing this was the end, embraced their parents, kissed each other, and vowed eternal faithfulness in whatever existence lies beyond the threshold of death.

Driver, horses, passengers: all of them drowned. The coach was never recovered. But, Greg's grandmother always told him, at midnight, under the light of an autumn moon, the spirit of the driver spurs the ghostly steeds with a hellish whip, and the carriage emerges from the depths, bearing its dead passengers into the world of the living once more.

By the time Greg was a senior in 1963, many people in and near

San Perlita claimed to have witnessed the ghastly apparition, including his uncle Jaime, who moved to San Antonio soon afterward. For many teens, it had become a test of courage to visit the lagoon late at night. So it was no surprise that on a clear fall evening, just after the homecoming game, Greg's friends Matt and Ronaldo tried to convince him to make the drive.

"Come on, man," Matt urged as they piled into his dented Ford Crestline. "It's not even that far from Raymondville."

"Yeah, Greg. Don't be so square. Or are you just scared?"

Reluctantly, Greg relented, and the three drove through the deepening darkness toward that haunted lagoon, the voice of Wolfman Jack rasping wildly from XERF-AM between rock and roll records. Then "Deep Purple" by Nino Tempo and April Stevens began to play, and Greg felt a shiver go up his spine as the siblings harmonized:

When the deep purple falls over sleepy garden walls
And the stars begin to twinkle in the sky—
In the mist of a memory, you wander back to me,
Breathing my name with a sigh...

"We should turn back," he muttered.

"Don't flip your wig, you flake." Ronaldo gestured ahead. "There's the trail. Pull over. Have to walk the rest of the way."

As April Stevens murmured "In the still of the night, once again I hold you tight," Greg shuddered and shut off the engine. The three got out and crept along the gravel road, twisted mesquite boughs arching overhead like the arms of hungry ghouls. Soon the sparse woods cleared, and there stretched the lagoon, its still waters deep purple beneath the silvery moonlight.

Matt and Ronaldo hurried to the shattered remains of a bridge, whitewashing all but worn away by the decades, and stood staring into the depths. Greg held back, nerves jangling. His friends made low noises of surprise.

"Hey, spaz, get over here!" Matt called out. "This is crazy, man."

His stomach was in knots, but Greg approached all the same. Looking into the water, he saw strange glints just below the surface, and deeper down glowing forms seemed to coalesce and dissolve.

"Some sort of fish," he mused, his voice trembling. "Scales reflecting the moonlight."

"I don't think so, panty waist." Ronaldo jerked his head. "You hear that sound? Like, hrm, muffled screams? Probably a bunch of..."

Without warning, water shot up in a hissing geyser, sending the young men stumbling backward. Greg tripped and fell flat on his back as clambering from the inky lagoon the bony forms of dead horses came, strips of rotting skin ribboning their muzzles and ribs. They neighed viciously as they pawed the air, dragging a waterlogged carriage from the depths. On the driver's bench sat a cadaveric fiend with glowing red eyes and a rictus of maddened glee: it wielded a fiery whip, lashing the skeletal steeds. From within the coach came the harrowing screams of the drowned, a chorus of damned, despairing voices.

Matt and Ronaldo had already begun running away at breakneck speed, but Greg had just dizzily regained his feet when the demonic driver looped that macabre cabriolet around. The doors opened, and the ghosts of both bride and groom emerged for a moment to embrace above the tattered roof...but then the horses plunged once more into the lagoon, and the driver gave a hellish laugh that echoed at Greg's heels all the way back to his car, to his home, in his dreams, and down the years to the present day.

Chupacabras in Mission

Most of us have seen artists' renditions of *chupacabras*: bizarre creatures with scaly grayish-green skin, large eyes that glow red in the darkness, stiletto-like fangs and sharp spines along their backs. Those who have seen the goatsuckers up-close claim they are about three to four feet tall, moving with unexpected quickness by hopping like a kangaroo. When startled or angry, the creatures hiss and make a chittering, whining sound. Most predators kill their prey; the chupacabras, however, drain all of an animal's blood through three holes in the shape of an upside-down triangle that they make with their teeth.

It's not clear if chupacabras are monsters from our own world or aliens from outer space. Whatever their origin may be, the chupacabras may have first appeared in 1975 in Puerto Rico. A large number of sheep were found dead that year, completely drained of their blood. People thought perhaps a vampire was responsible. Twenty years later, the killings started again, with goats and sheep and pets being sucked dry, each with three puncture wounds on its chest or neck. A woman named Madelyne Tolentino became the first eyewitness, and her description has been confirmed repeatedly ever since.

By the early 2000s, the creatures had made their way to the rest of Latin America. One of the worst attacks by bands of chupacabras occurred in July and August of 2010: more than 300 goats in and around the city of Zapotitlán in the state of Puebla had their throats ripped out and their blood drained. Ranchers from the area, along with local and state police, were unable to track the monsters down and destroy them.

Around that same time, the fertile land and sturdy livestock of South Texas apparently drew a group of the bloodsucking creatures to the area. They preyed upon many local ranches, most notably the Lozano family spread north of Mission, just off of Highway 107.

Francisco Lozano had heard the complaints of neighboring

ranchers: sick cows, dead calves, missing chickens. None of those problems was particularly surprising, of course. As long as mankind has been involved in animal husbandry, he has faced such losses again and again. When people whispered the word "chupacabras," Francisco simply shrugged.

"Maybe," he would concede, having been taught that the world was more mysterious than people ever imagine, "but probably not."

But as the winter of 2009-2010 swept cool winds and rain into the Valley, animals on the Lozano ranch began to die.

At first these were deer and jackrabbits that Francisco stumbled across as he toured the edges of his land. Their bodies had often begun to decompose and to be picked at by vultures, so the cause of death was uncertain. There was little to no blood around the otherwise uneaten flesh, which seemed to dash any theory about free-ranging cougars on the prowl.

A few coyotes turned up dead as well before the predator closed in on the family's livestock. A dozen or so chickens went missing; a prized goat as well, though its bones would be discovered months later on a neighbor's property.

Francisco and his sons tried all they could to keep a vigil, certain that they could kill whatever beast had targeted their animals. But despite their efforts, the family was shocked to discover one of their cows lying dead in the pasture one morning.

The body was still slightly warm when Francisco examined it. He found an odd triangular arrangement of puncture wounds on its neck and strange claw marks on its flanks.

"El chupacabras," whispered his eldest son in awe and horror.

"Hush, now, boy. Go get your horse and some rope. We can't eat this meat."

While his son hurried to comply, Francisco imagined the ghastly beast knocking the cow down, digging its alien talons deep into that brown hide, sinking stiletto fangs into the carotid and drinking deep till the heifer stilled her struggle and succumbed to creeping death.

I must stop this thing before it takes all my cattle, he thought as his son returned astride his gelding. Together they dragged the corpse deep into the brush so that nature could reclaim its flesh through scavengers and heat and chemical change.

Taking turns at watch, a bonfire blazing all night, Francisco Lozano and his sons managed to keep the remaining animals safe. Gradually, the corpses of wild animals stopped appearing even at the edges of the ranch, and the family breathed a sigh of relief. They had outlasted the eerie predator.

A long, hot summer was burning into its final September days when Francisco met his *compadre* at the gate to the ranch. This life-long friend had been wanting to hunt white-wing for years, and today the two of them had agreed to spend the morning trekking through the brush in hopes of bagging a few of the migrating doves.

Shortly after noon, each having shot his legal quota, the friends headed back to their trucks, shotguns empty and broken over the crook of their arms.

As they neared the entrance to the ranch, a horrifying shape squeezed its way through the gate. Bluish-green reptilian skin stretched taut across a bony, emaciated but wiry body. Long hind legs ground prehensile claws into the sand earth, tensing for a leap. Along the knobby ridge of the creature's spine, black quills jutted viciously, a dangerous line that terminated at the sleek, almost canine head. Red eyes turned on the hunters, and the black lips pulled back in a hideous snarl.

Francisco hesitated for just the space of a heartbeat. Then he yanked two shells from his camouflaged vest, rammed them into the breach, clicked his shotgun closed with expert speed and fired both barrels at the monster just as it leapt into the air.

It sprawled in the withered sage, dead.

"Mother of God!" Francisco's compadre exclaimed with respectful wonderment. "You just killed a chupacabras."

"Yup."

"No one's going to believe us, Frank."

"Not till they see for themselves. Help me lug this sucker to my truck. We'll see what the experts say."

Wincing a little at the feel of that slick, alien hide, the two of them lifted the carcass and tossed into the bed of the pick-up.

Even if they don't believe, thought Francisco as he clicked the tailgate closed, *even if the university folks say this ain't a* chupacabras *at all, I protected my family and my ranch. No more danger to them.*

In the end, he knew, and that was what really mattered.

The Flying Witch of Monterrey

Since the time of the Mayan kingdoms, witches have been feared and respected in Mexico. These men and women have for thousands of years used spells and other means to manipulate *teotl*, spiritual energy, to accomplish their goals. Depending on what those goals are, their magic is considered either white or black. White witches usually prefer some other label: *curandero, shaman, granicero, santero.* For most people in Mexico and the US Southwest, the Spanish word “bruja” (probably derived from the Latin “*plusscia*” or “knowledgeable”) is immediately associated with black magic and evil deeds.

Witches are typically female (though there are *brujos* aplenty in border lore). They use rituals, spells, incantations, potions, and powders to work ill against others: the evil eye, physical or mental illness, bad luck, or even death. When a physician using modern medical equipment and knowledge can’t cure someone who has suddenly gotten sick, a witch is immediately blamed. The family may hire a curandero to 'undo' whatever evil spell has twisted the victim’s health, to protect the person and to restore balance.

Since pre-Columbian times, Mexican witches have also been considered shape shifters, possessing the supernatural ability to transform themselves into owls, coyotes, jaguars, etc. In their animal forms, they can spy on potential victims and attack them without notice, adding a potion to the person’s food or water, hiding a hex bag or charm near or on the victim. Certain medallions or rituals are said to protect you from witches. If you suspect one is after you, you may want to talk to a priest, pastor or *curandero.* You might need their services.

For more than a century, women dressed in black have been sighted flying through the hills of Nuevo León, Mexico. Though these reports are often dismissed, recent evidence suggests there may indeed be at least one flying witch near Monterrey.

Witches are said to travel through the night air in three ways: in the form of a bird, usually a screech owl; on a broomstick, a trick they learned from their European cousins; or as a ball of fire that moves quickly through the air. Many rituals, including the exorcism known as *The Twelve Truths*, are said to bring a flying witch down. The surest way to do so, however, is to put your clothes on backwards and recite the *Apostles' Creed* in Latin, also backwards, word for word. The ball of fire or owl will supposedly fall from the sky when you're done, and when you search you'll find the backbone of a cow lying on the ground. Tie it to a tree. In the morning, when the sun rises, the witch will be there it its place.

Police officer Leonardo Samaniego of Guadalupe, Nuevo León, Mexico, had been taught all these spine-tingling facts about witches when he was a little boy. But when he finally came face to face with a bruja, panic and fear made him forget his grandmother's lessons.

At 3:15 AM on Friday, January 16, 2004, Samaniego was doing his rounds in his patrol car around Colonia Valles de la Silla. The night was cold and dark and the streets were empty when Samaniego made a turn onto Alamo Street. Suddenly a large black mass fell from a tree that overhung the street, stopping a foot or so from the ground and hovering for a second before gradually lowering to the blacktop.

The shadowy form turned and faced the patrol car. Samaniego struggled to make out its identity. Was it a drunk? Some wayward punk looking to tag private property with a can of spray paint? Maybe a burglar or cartel mule? After squinting a few seconds, the officer flipped on his high beams.

It was a woman, decked out entirely in black: dress, cape, pointed hat. She stood stock still for several moments, staring at Samaniego, visibly irritated by the bright lights. Then the witch—for what else could it be?—exploded into movement, leaping onto the hood of Samaniego's patrol car and slamming the butt of her broom handle repeatedly against the windshield. The shocked police officer threw the car into reverse and floored the gas pedal. While glancing frantically over his shoulder to navigate, he lifted his radio with shaking hands and called out in desperation for back-up.

The witch lost her grip on the broom and screamed in frustra-tion. As the car lurched backward in an erratic zigzag, she crouched and continued to beat at the glass with her claw-like hands. Samaniego noticed the woman's eyes were abnormally big and totally black, without even eyelids. Her mouth opened wide as she howled with rage, and her face twisted horribly.

When Samaniego's patrol car finally slammed into the curb at the end of the street, its engine clattering till it stalled, the officer was so overcome with shock that he simply passed out.

When other police and paramedics arrived, they found Samaniego unconscious but uninjured, probably because he never left his vehicle. Once the officer had recovered enough to speak, a camera operator on site recorded his first interview. In talking to his dubious colleagues, Samaniego insisted that he'd been attacked by a flying witch.

Though investigators found no additional physical evidence or trace of the purported *bruja, v*ideo of the windshield—dented and deeply scored by the woman's claws—has been suppressed by authorities.

Two years later, a group of UFO enthusiasts in Monterrey, captured on camera a strange figure crossing the sky in a straight line. The recording shows a silhouette in the shape of a woman with a pointy head and hunchback posture: she has been dubbed "the flying witch of Monterrey."

When asked to confirm whether the figure in the video was the same that attacked him, Officer Samaniego simply covered his eyes and stammered, "No comment!"

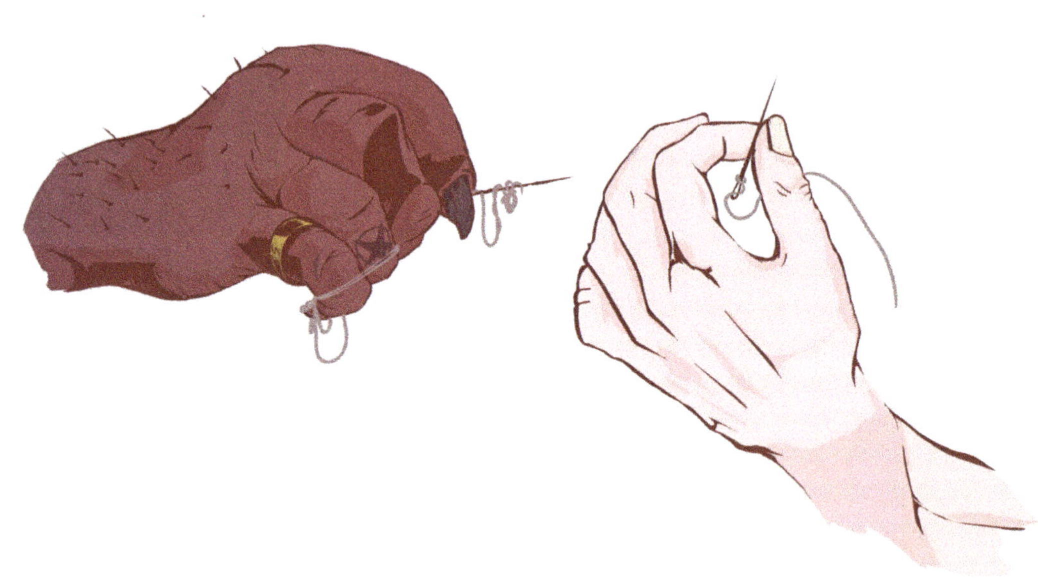

The Virgin Mary Versus Satan

The old folks tell us that there is a long-standing rivalry between the Devil and the Virgin Mary, destined by prophecy to crush that old snake's head. Many times down the millennia he has tried to get the upper hand, but Mary shows the greater skill and strength time and time again.

One day Satan found himself sick to death of the reputation Mary had for being the best seamstress in the universe. Hadn't he, the morning star, helped fashion the very cosmos before his fall? It was unthinkable that this once mortal woman should show him up this way.

He found the Queen of Heaven watching over her children on earth, and he approached with his accustomed slyness.

"Mother, I have heard your hands are steady and sure, but I wager I can sew better and faster than you."

With a beatific smile, Mary looked at him and gave the slightest of nods. "Very well. I accept your challenge, Lucifer."

As the hosts of heaven and hell gathered round to witness the contest, each took up thimble, needle and thread. The signal was given to begin, and Mary cut a small length of thread and slipped it through the eye of her needle.

"Oh, foolish woman," cried the Devil. "You'll take forever that way!"

Laughing, he unspooled his thread without cutting it till it spilled in loops around his hooves.

But though Mary took her time and patiently used shorter sections, her infernal opponent found himself going slower because his thread snarled and knotted constantly, causing him to stop and untangle it.

In the end, the Virgin completed her task first, and the angels rejoiced. Dejected, Satan had no choice but to declare her the winner there before all of creation.

And that was the lesson my grandmother taught her daughters: patience and small sections so your thread does not snarl.

Sound advice for sewing as well as for life itself.

The Headless Horseman of South Texas

In late 1968, Samuel Dresch stood drinking rot-gut liquor in the middle of the night, staring out at the moonlit mesquite trees of his grandfather's ranch north of McAllen. His marriage was just days away; not long after the brief honeymoon, he would be shipping off to Vietnam. Pensive, unable to fully enjoy his last moments of freedom, the young man dreamed of being an outlaw, of throwing fiancée and draft card to the wind and living a life of hedonism and crime.

At that moment, a rider came thundering through the brush. Startled, Samuel dropped his flask and took several steps back till he bumped into a gnarled ash. He could not believe his eyes.

Upon a blood-red mustang rode a figure dressed in black, with bandoliers strapped across its chest in a silvered X, nickel handles of revolvers glinting beneath the sallow moon. Gloved hands and booted feet guided the snorting steed with practiced ease, flicking reins and touching wicked spurs to scarred flanks.

But Samuel scarcely registered these details.

For, you see, the horseman's head did not sit upon its shoulders; instead, it hung from the saddle by leather thongs, strapped within a bangled sombrero that bounced horrifically with every stride.

Samuel Dresch bolted for his truck and never looked back. He married, did his tour in Vietnam, and moved wife and newborn as far from the Valley as he could.

He was neither the first nor last to see this headless horse-man. For some one hundred and fifty years the figure, known to locals as *el Muerto*, has roamed the Tamaulipan brushland along the Rio Grande. Many tales have been told of his origins, most crediting his decapitation to Texas Rangers Bigfoot Wallace and Creed Taylor.

As is often the case, history is much stranger than the legend.

The man who would become *el Muerto* was born Adrián Vidal in Monterrey, Nuevo León, Mexico in 1840 to Colonel Luis Vidal and his wife

Petra Vela. When the colonel died a decade later, Petra moved with her five children to Mier, a small Mexican town on the border. Without his father around to guide him, Adrián grew wild, running with a street gang and partaking at an early age of a wide range of vices.

In 1852 Mifflin Kenedy, steamboating and ranching partner of the infamous Richard King, was visiting Mier on business when the still beautiful Petra caught his eye. They were married shortly thereafter, and Adrián found himself and his siblings living on Kenedy's expansive lands near Brownsville.

Resentful of his stepfather and uneasy in his new life, Adrián plunged deeper into the underbelly of border society, garnering a reputation by his mid-teens as a fighter, a gambler, a drunkard, and a faithful customer of houses of ill repute. Much of his destructive behavior stemmed from his grief over the loss of his father. Obsessed with contacting the colonel beyond the grave, the adolescent fell in with practitioners of the dark arts: wizards and mediums, witches and necromancers. He delved into knowledge that no man should have.

By the time he was twenty-one, Adrián Vidal was feared and reviled by decent folk. Then the Civil War broke out, and the young man saw an opportunity to engage in his vices elsewhere.

Traveling to San Antonio, he joined the Confederate army and was promoted in short order from private to lieutenant. Sent back to the border with a company of men his knowledge of the area had earned him, Lieutenant Vidal began the work of preventing Union incursions at the mouth of the river. His greatest victory was capturing a gunboat sent by Northern forces, a gambit that garnered him a captaincy.

Vidal chafed, however, under the military yoke of orders and insufficient materiel, so in 1863 he and his men mutinied, going from Confederate fighters to hardened outlaws. General Hamilton Bee sent two soldiers to bring Vidal back for court martial, but he attacked them immediately, killing Private D. H. Dashiell, the son of the Texas Adjutant General. The other man escaped with serious wounds and informed his superiors of the ambush.

There was nothing holding Vidal back now: the entire Confederate Army wanted him dead, so he threw himself into his role as bandit. With his gang of deserters he pillaged, raped, killed and raided ranches, stealing horses even from the likes of Texas Rangers Creed Taylor and William "Big Foot" Wallace, who swore they'd kill the outlaw and harried him across

South Texas until he sought refuge in Mexico.

The pickings were leaner south of the Rio Grande, so in time Vidal brought his band back to Texas, where the North had just seized control of the Nueces Strip. Enlisting in the Union forces as *Vidal's Independent Partisan Rangers,* the sly bandits "patrolled" an area that stretched west to Roma and north to the Nueces.

Of course, Union military hierarchy was no different from that of the Confederate Army, and Vidal soon was fed up with bureaucracy and slights against his cultural heritage. He attempted to resign in May of 1864, but when no response was forthcoming, he and his men once more abandoned their post and headed for Mexico, where they join Juan Cortina as that famous rebel fought against the imperialist forces of Maximillian in hopes of reinstalling Benito Juárez as president.

Vidal waged a brutal campaign, summarily executing every enemy soldier he captured. When at last he was taken by imperialist troops in the town of Camargo, the military trial concluded that he was a deadly and unreasoning threat against the Mexican Empire.

Mifflin Kenedy learned of his stepson's capture and rushed to propose a hefty ransom, telegramming his intent immediately. But the imperialists understood that no sum was worth freeing the vicious and cruel enemy they had in their grasp. They sentenced him to death by firing squad.

"Kill me then," Vidal spat. "Death is no barrier for men like me, you dogs. I will rise from my grave before the month is out and harry you to the ends of the earth!"

Shaken by his mad and gleeful promise, the troops emptied several dozen volleys into his flesh and then decapitated his corpse for good measure.

Kenedy arrived to find his stepson dead and desecrated. With little ceremony, he transported the remains back to Brownsville and buried them.

And when the next full moon wavered upon the water of the Rio Grande, a wild mustang galloped into the cemetery and stood twitching by the grave of Adrián Vidal. From that freshly settled earth a hand burst, clutching a handsome but diabolic head by its long black hair.

The Headless Horseman of South Texas emerged into the moonlight and mounted his steed.

The Sack Man

The Sack Man is a bogeyman who haunts neighborhoods in Mexico and the US Southwest. The old-timers call him *el hombre del saco* or *el viejo del costal*, describing the Sack Man as quite old, very mean, and horribly ugly. A bag thrown over his back, this skinny bald villain shows up on the streets around suppertime, on the lookout for disobedient children who didn't go inside when their mothers called them to the table. As the sun sets on these unsuspecting naughty kids, the Sack Man approaches them slyly; most run away screaming, but some think he's just a hobo and tease him for his dirty, disheveled appearance. He smiles a toothy smile and undrapes the bag, swinging it through the air to trap the child within. Once inside the complete blackness of that sack, there is no escape. The Sack Man carries his burden home, whistling contentedly. Then he eats the kid.

Most people who tell the tale have no idea why the Sack Man feels compelled to kill and devour children. However, some researchers claim to have found his origins in the chilling case of the vampire of Gádor.

In the Spanish province of Almeria, that part of Andalusia where so many spaghetti Westerns have been filmed, the small town of Gádor sits nestled beside a megalithic necropolis, ancient graves dating from the Bronze Age.

It was in this sleepy but somber hamlet that in 1910 a middle-aged man of means named Francisco Ortega discovered he was dying of tuberculosis. Having tried every cure imaginable, Ortega turned in desperation to a gypsy witch, Augustina Rodríguez.

"Ah," she told him with a sad smile, "such disease is beyond my humble talents. But go to my colleague Paco Leona, *el Barbero*, and he will surely have an answer."

Leona was a *curandero* of dubious reputation, but Ortega was at his wits' end. He found the old barber in a tavern, drinking steadily despite his seventy-five years.

"You've come to the right fellow," Leona grunted after hearing his plea. "I know exactly how to rid your body of the white plague. Question is, can you stand the horror?"

"Don Paco, I'm willing to do anything you say! I don't want to die, do you understand?"

The barber leaned across the table, whispering through his yellow, broken teeth: "You have to drink the blood of an innocent and smear your chest with fat from his flesh."

Ortega jerked away, crossing himself in shock. "What a monstrous thing to suggest! You're mad, Barber. Completely mad!"

Outraged, the sick man left. But as the weeks went by and his illness worsened, he found himself on his knees, coughing up black blood, crying out to a heaven that never responded.

He could see no alternative beyond the horrible death he feared.

Paco Leona welcomed Ortega into his dilapidated home with a toothy smile. "I take it you've reconsidered, then?"

Swallowing heavily, Ortega nodded. "But I...I can't possibly... *procure* a child myself."

"No, no. Nor should you. No idea what do look for, anyway. No, you leave that to me. Just bring me 3,000 *reales* and I'll take care of the sordid details, friend."

Leona enlisted the help of Julio *el Tonto* Hernández, son of the gypsy witch who had first recommended the services of *el Barbero* to Ortega. Together the men kidnapped seven-year-old Bernardo González from the nearby town of Rioja, stuffing him inside a burlap sack and taking him back to Gádor. Making a cut under the young boy's arm, they bled him to death. Leona then scraped away what little fat could be found on the skinny child's corpse.

Word was sent to Ortega that it was time for his cure. He arrived at the home of the *curandero*, handed over the substantial sum of money, and was given a mixture of blood and sugar to drink. The fat was applied in compresses to the sick man's chest.

Within twenty-four hours, he could breathe normally. His pallid skin returned to its natural swarthy complexion. His cough had disappeared, and he found he had an appetite for food once again.

Perhaps my soul is damned, he thought, but my last years on earth will be spent hale and whole.

After three weeks, however, his illness returned. Bewildered and furious, he confronted Paco Leona.

"Ah, there's the rub, eh? The cure is temporary, friend. You'll need to do this every month if you want to enjoy good health."

"I can't spend 3,000 *reales* a month! My meager savings would be soon depleted, Barber."

"Then I guess you'll have to do the kidnapping and killing yourself, won't you?" snarled the old man.

As Ortega pondered his dilemma, though, other complications arose. Leona was supposed to have shared his fee with Julio and the witch, but he'd come up with a thousand excuses, trying to wrangle a larger share for himself. Julio finally tired of these games and reported seeing a boy's corpse near Las Pocicas, where he and Paco had abandoned the body. Proving the aptness of his nickname, Julio *el Tonto* mangled his story badly, and instead of getting just Paco arrested, he put himself and most of his family in prison as well.

Learning of the developments, Francisco Ortega panicked. He fled to Almeria City, the closest port, and managed to buy himself passage across the Atlantic.

A few weeks later, he kidnapped his first Latin-American victim. And, the old-timers say, he has never stopped killing since.

So, the story goes, the Sack Man was born, wandering the Western Hemisphere, kept alive like some twisted vampire by the blood of the innocent. He targets badly behaved children or those abandoned by their parents, thinking these victims deserve or want death. But he is a monster nonetheless. There is no real protection against him, unfortunately, except obedience and love.

The Ghosts of Fort Ringgold

It was a late spring morning in 1990 when 8th-graders Arturo Sandoval and Leticia Blanco slipped from their middle-school campus in Rio Grande City, having decided the day was too beautiful and they were too much in love to be sitting through mathematics and science. Leti was a little nervous about skipping class, but they managed to evade the cursory watch kept by teachers and administrators in order to make their escape.

"It ain't far," Art said as the campus receded behind them. "Just act natural. Quit looking all around, babe."

"I can't help it. My dad'll kill me if we get caught."

"We ain't getting caught. I swear it." He took her hand in his and smiled. Leti swallowed her fear and smiled back.

Soon they had made it through the meager camouflage of mesquites clumped along a block of Clay Davies Street in what remained of old Fort Ringgold, its buildings and barracks adapted down the years for use by the school district. Emerging onto a parking lot, they quickly scurried between two steel buildings and stared from the shade.

There it stood on a low hill carpeted by unnaturally green grass, clapboards almost leprous with peeling white paint and black dots of rot: the Robert E. Lee House, its strange double roof hunch-ing down against the ever-warming sun.

"They say General Lee lived here back in 1860," Leti whispered, nearly in awe. "He came to deal with Juan Cortina and all the raids he was doing."

Art shrugged. "Girl, Cortina was a freaking hero. Dude was trying to stop oppression and stuff. Like Robin Hood and César Chávez rolled into one. You never heard his *corrido*? My *tío* has it on cassette. It's *bad*. Besides, who cares what some slave-loving general did?"

"This was before the Confederacy, Arturito. He was still working for the US military."

The boy shrugged. "*Chale*. Whatever."

Hand in hand, they dashed to the historical landmark.

"Come on, get on through," Art instructed, lifting the fence up where it had been clipped a few years back. He squeezed in after her.

They mounted the hill together and climbed the steps to the porch that ran along the outside of the old home. Art's friends had told him which window could be opened, and the couple was soon inside the stuffy gloom, leaning against each other as light slanted through the room in dusty beams.

Leti clinging to Art's arm, the adolescents toured the empty house in silence. It was pretty unremarkable; tenants living there during the past hundred years had remodeled its interior many times, so it didn't seem antiquated, merely old.

They stopped in the kitchen, and Art leaned in to give his girl a kiss.

"No, don't. I'm nervous. They say this place is haunted."

He waved her fears away. "*Puro cuento*. Grown-ups say that stuff so kids won't come here. But my friends ain't ever seen a ghost, babe, and they been here lots of times."

Leti pulled away from his embrace. "Yeah, well, all of this used to be old Fort Ringgold, and my *abuela* says the spirits of the fallen soldiers still roam the place, especially the unknown soldier."

Art smirked at her. "Babe, even the teachers say that's all lies. Last year, when you were still up in Minnesota, Mr. Reyes took us on a field trip to look for the grave of *ese mentado* unknown soldier. But Reyes said the dude wasn't a soldier. He told the class that like in 1888 this jerk named Sebree, friend of the white sheriff, killed a Mexican-American prisoner 'cause supposably he was trying to escape. Yeah, right. Sebree had already lynched other Mexicans, so everybody got super mad and started rioting."

Leti nodded. "Sure, I know the story. Even though the townspeople finally broke up and went home, folks around the country were scared at a bunch of us demonstrating like that."

"And they sent more troops. So people died. That's who Reyes said is in that tomb. Not some unknown soldier, but the last rioter, which he got himself executed by a firing squad 'cause he shot somebody important."

Leti shivered. The kitchen had gotten suddenly cold.

"No matter what the truth is, Arturito, their spirits could still be trapped here. Let's go back to school."

"And get sent to the principal's office? *Chale, flaca.*"

He bent to kiss her again, oblivious to the misty breath that curled from both their mouths.

"Don't be afraid. I ain't letting no ghost mess with you."

At his words, all the cabinet doors in the kitchen burst open. Drawers pistoned in and out in jerky, syncopated rhythm. The floorboards beneath the couple's feet began to groan.

Leti screamed in horror.

Seizing his girlfriend by the arm, Art pulled her from the kitchen. They ran through the house toward the room with the unblocked window, but the door slammed in their faces. The base-board along one wall whipped away with a snapping sound, nearly crashing into Arturo's head.

Soon the whole house was shaking, a frigid wind slashing back and forth through its empty yet haunted spaces. Arturo pounded and kicked at the door to no avail.

Leti, her heart thudding, suddenly had an idea. She stepped into the center of the living room and began to speak.

"We...we're sorry to come without permission. We know you're mad. It...it wasn't fair, what happened to you. It was an injustice, a tragedy. But listen: *somos de los suyos*. We're one of you, okay? Let us leave, and we'll honor you. We'll let people know that good men and women were killed in this town for speaking their minds. We won't let them forget you."

The cold air seemed to fall still for a moment, then it compressed with an audible *whoosh* till there before the youngsters in the living room floated the glowing, silvered contours of a man. He stared at them with icy eyes for a moment, then turned and gestured at the door.

It opened onto the sunny warmth of early afternoon.

The poltergeist was letting them go.

Once outside, Art hurried away, anxious to put the house and its ghostly inhabitant behind him. But Leti couldn't help but turn back once more. The revenant drifted faintly in the shadows of the porch, features twisted with a century's worth of grief and indignation.

Leticia Blanco couldn't bear the sight. Burying her face in her hands, the girl wept for all the fallen innocents of the world.

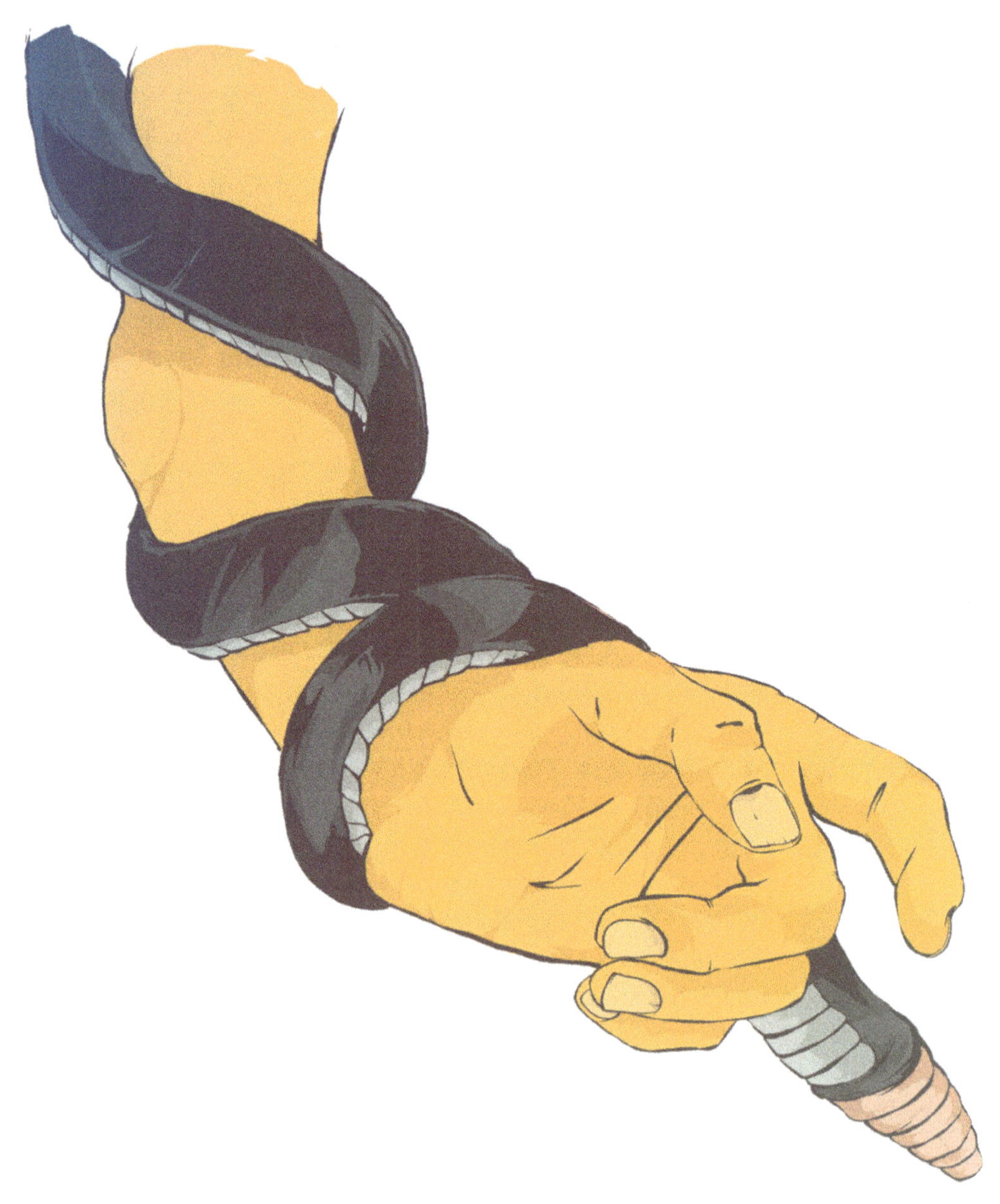

Alicante

The old folks say that the *alicante* doesn't move like other snakes: instead of dragging itself along on its belly, it holds itself as straight as possible, balanced on the end of its tail. When it sees likely food—a mouse or rat, for example—it leaps through the air toward its victim, returning immediately to its upright, cobra-like pose.

The scariest thing about the alicante is that it likes human milk. This reptile prefers to hunt at night, so it will often slip its way into the warmth of a house in those cooler hours. If it discovers a mother breast-feeding a newborn, the snake begins making a low, whistling sound that hypnotizes her. Once she is deep in a trance, the alicante shakes the rattle at the end of its tail, distracting the baby as it leaps onto the bed. As it begins to drink milk from the mother, it lets the baby play with its tail, even putting the rattle in the infant's mouth to keep it from crying in frustration and hunger.

But human milk is not always available, so the alicante will call to cows and goats with its seductive whistle, attaching itself to their udders once it has herded them close. Many a rancher has been completely unnerved by the sight of a snake dangling from his prize dairy cow in the early morning hours.

Sometime in the late 1800s, a young couple living on La Blanca Ranch had a harrowing encounter with an alicante. Juan and Martha Barquero noticed that their newborn son just could not thrive, despite all the milk his mother was producing. The sickly baby seemed to grow thinner and thinner, and all around his chapped lipped strange welts had begun to rise.

The Barqueros tried everything they could, from family remedies to desperate experiments. Nothing worked. They borrowed enough money to entice a doctor to visit their home, but he was at a loss as to what the problem could be.

At their wits' end, the couple traveled to the home of a reclusive *cuandera* and explained their concerns. After examining the baby, the wise woman nodded.

"Your son is not ill," he told them. "He has been displaced by an alicante. Go straight home, Juan, and look at the rafters above your bed. You will undoubtedly find a serpent there, fat and drowsy. It has been feeding on Martha's milk at night, slithering down from the ceiling and using its silent rattle-tipped tail to keep the baby quiet. You will have to kill it, quickly, or it will find its way back inside."

Horrified, the couple hurried back to their humble *jacal*. Cautiously, Juan probed the beams with a stick until a hissing whistle signaled the presence of the thieving viper. It dropped onto the bed, coiling blackly before jerking itself erect and baring its fangs.

"Come on, filthy reptile!" shouted Juan, brandishing his machete. "No one touch my son and lives!"

The alicante leaped through the air at the young man, who slashed with his blade and cut the creature in two. Another blow beheaded it. He took the remains outside and burned them.

In time, the baby's health improved, and he grew fat and content.

As a grown man, however, he could never overcome his fear of snakes.

The Sea Monster of Port Isabel

When Charlotte Barnard agreed to marry James Sewell after a short courtship, she didn't do so just out of love or because James was manager of a chain of oil refineries along the Texas coast. Of course, she did feel great attraction for the dashing Texan and his healthy financial prospects, but it was instead a sense of destiny that drew her away from her native Syracuse and toward the Lone Star State, a tickle at the back of her mind that suggested great things awaited.

As a child and teen, Charlotte had gone fishing with her father nearly every weekend on the rivers and lakes of New York State, and by the time of her marriage in 1935, she had spent a good chunk of her twenty-eight years yanking bass, drum and sturgeon from the depths of Oneida and Onandaga. As a result, once she and her husband were installed in their sturdy home in Bayview at the very tip of Texas, she immediately began indulging her hobby in these new environs. Starting with gulf trout and channel bass, robalo and salt-water pike, she mastered the fine points of bay fishing in little more than a year.

But bigger game was waiting. Charlotte learned of the annual Rio Grande Valley Fishing Rodeo, and she felt certain she could sweep the women's division. James bought a yacht, the couple hired a captain, and Charlotte started to train on the open sea beyond South Padre Island.

In August of 1937, Charlotte was ready. Though many fishermen and tougher-looking women raised eyebrows at her slim 5'2" frame, the Syracuse native scanned the sea with an uncanny sense for the denizens of its depths. Soon she had boated a 7-foot-6-inch sailfish, deflating the egos of her competitors as she was awarded the 200-dollar prize in front of one of the largest crowds ever to attend the ceremony.

The following year, though the Sewells had moved to San Benito, Charlotte was ready to up the ante, perhaps even to gaff a blue marlin, the holy grail of deep-sea fishing in South Texas.

Then the rumors starting coming in: Mexican fishing boats were encountering some strange leviathan, looming ominously just below the surface of the sea. The Brownsville Herald reported the story, and many contestants considered withdrawing just days before the rodeo began.

Charlotte Sewell took all the paranoia with a grain of salt till the day in mid-August when a boat came careening into port, smacking up against pylons before men and boys dropped from its decks in a panic.

Stopping one sun-baked youngster, she asked in halting Spanish, "*¿Qué pasa*?"

"*Un monstruo*," the boy replied breathlessly. "We see a monster. *Medía unos cuarenta metros de largo*. Forty!" He stretched his arms wide to emphasize the gargantuan size.

The boy in tow, Charlotte soon verified the sighting with other members of the crew. Little Carlos had been telling the truth. A massive bulk had passed directly under the boat, ripping free the nets and diving with a full day's catch.

Now she was intrigued. "Forty feet long," she told her competitors, both men and women. "That's what the boy said. Can you imagine catching something as massive? Now *that* would be a feat for the record books."

Several agreed, and they convinced the captain of the fishing boat to take them out to where the beast had been sighted. They equipped the vessel with harpoons and 500 feet of rope to which they attached dozens of tightly plugged barrels. The idea was to spear the monstrosity and keep it from sounding so that it could be hauled back to the Laguna Madre.

Several other ships set out on the sea monster's trail, including the cabin cruiser *Andrey,* captained by B.B. Burnell and carrying the mayor and other prominent citizens. The Coast Guard decided to keep a protective eye on the expedition, local commander Pablo Valent assuring the media that boats would be at the ready to render aid to all who required it.

The hunt lasted days. Charlotte hardly slept; instead, she sat near the prow, feet propped on the gunwale, scanning the waves. But after the better part of a week, there was still no sign of any gargantuan creature. The rag-tag expedition headed back into port. Many captains blamed Charlotte for getting folks riled up and wasting their time; Burnell, on the other hand, expressed confidence that the monster would reappear someday.

Charlotte managed her chagrin and the cold looks of her peers by throwing herself into the competition the following week, once again snatching first prize from the hands of more seasoned women.

Interest in the supposed monster waned, its existence dismissed as a hoax or explained away as sightings of whale sharks. Charlotte couldn't shake the thought that there was something more, however. The look on Carlos's face as he'd sprinted away from the ship was scored into her memory. She spent much of the autumn of 1938 and spring of 1939 on her yacht, fishing for marlin and hoping to come across the strange, formless bulk that haunted her dreams.

She took second place that August, losing to Mrs. Duemler of Dallas. Pregnancy kept her off the sea, and as Hitler swept westward through Europe, the tournament struck Charlotte as a little frivolous. Perhaps it was time to ease back on the intensity of her hobby, as James was always begging her.

One more year, she told herself. One more try at winning the open competition, at going head-to-head with the men and beating them soundly on behalf of all women. Then I'll while away my days, teaching my children to fish along rivers and channels.

The tournament was a disaster. Charlotte didn't even place. The scrawny sailfish she snagged might as well have been returned to the depths for all the points it garnered her.

But as she and her crew moored the little yacht in its berth, a young man came running up to her, calling out breathlessly.

"Señora Sewell! It's me, remember?" It was Carlos, now a strapping teen.

"Of course, dear. What's wrong? You seem upset."

"The monster. We see him again. This time, knock over a boat. We come back for harpoons and help. You help?"

She hesitated. It was madness, this idea of going out in search of a sea monster again. But the boy's wide eyes and trembling limbs told her something truly awe-inspiring plied the Gulf waters, and she simply couldn't turn away from a chance to reel it in.

"Yes, Carlos. I'll help."

Less than a day later, her yacht arrived with three fishing boats to the wreckage that floated a dozen nautical miles or so off shore. The wind stilled as everyone scanned the shattered timbers for signs of the predator. Crews tossed chum onto the low swells, hoping to lure it to the surface.

Just as Charlotte was beginning to suspect that this hunt would be as fruitless as the last, a white form twice the length of her yacht streamed through the water to starboard.

"It's here!" she shouted, turning to Carlos, who had agreed to sail with her. "Forty feet long, just like you said!"

Carlos shook his head. "No, señora. Not that. Big shark, not monster. *Y no son cuarenta pies. Cuarenta* metros. Forty *yards*."

"What?" Charlotte swung her eyes back to the water. A white whale shark broke the surface, skimming the chum.

And then, with a rushing roar like some mad typhoon, a horrifying cyclopean form burst from the sea, snatching the shark in unearthly jaws as it rose higher and higher above the ships. Waves slammed against the yacht, spinning it like a top. Charlotte clung to the gunwale and gaped in shock. Sickly green, groping at the hot air with what seemed branches or tentacles, the massive leviathan seemed to hover for a moment, looming like some twisted antediluvian god, neither plant nor animal but something vastly more ancient. Then it fell back into the water, creating a tsunami of sorts that capsized one boat and sent the others rushing back toward land.

When the yacht limped back into port, Charlotte Sewell disembarked without a word and went home to hug her son tightly. That evening she told James she wanted to move.

"Dallas would be good, or San Antonio. Some place far from the coast."

And she never returned to the sea.

Ghost Tracks of San Antonio

On April 7, 1991, the word spread like wildfire throughout south Texas: Selena Quintanilla was putting on a free charity concert in San Antonio, outdoors at the Market Square. Oscar Garza, who wasn't actually a big fan of Selena, nonetheless immediately called his girlfriend Río Villanueva.

"Babe," he breathed into the phone. "You sitting down?"

"Yes, Oscar. I'm fixing my hair, getting ready to drive to Pan Am."

"Well, you're going to want to ditch your Friday classes, Río."

"*Not*," she quipped sarcastically. "I've got a test, sweetie."

"Trust me, you'll blow it off. Selena y los Dinos. Tonight. San Antonio. I'm taking you and the rest of the guys."

"No way!"

Oscar smiled and did his best Bill and Ted impression: "Yes way!"

Squealing with excitement, Rio hung up to get ahold of Melody Sánchez while Oscar contacted his best friends, Javier Vásquez and Luis Serrano. By about 1 pm the five of them were on the road, radio blaring, laughter and conversation filling every nook and cranny of Oscar's beat-up and dusty Chevy Cavalier (nicknamed "The Smurfmobile" by the rest of the group because of its bright blue paintjob). For most of the group, this was the end of their freshman year at college, and they definitely needed a break.

None of them had any money to speak of, but that hardly mattered. They pooled their change, filled the tank, and hit highway 281. They stopped a couple of times for bathroom breaks, everyone laughing at the defective child locks that made Oscar have to open the back doors like a chauffeur.

"Thank you, Jeeves," they would quip in bad British accents. Oscar smiled and went along with their ribbing. Among friends, being the brunt of a joke isn't so bad.

Though they got to San Antonio early, the square was already packed. By the time the band took up their instruments, more than a thousand people had crammed themselves together to hear la Reina del Tex-Mex. Los Dinos, wearing black and white costumes designed by the singer, struck up the first tune, an unexpected cover of "Everybody, Everybody" by Black Box. Selena came dancing out onto the stage, and the crowd went wild, including Río, whose screaming nearly deafened Oscar.

Working their way through some of her most beloved songs, the young vocalist enthralled the fans, returning after the last number, "Dame un beso," in order to perform Russell Hitchcock's "Where Did the Feeling Go?" as an encore.

Exhausted but euphoric, the five friends made their way back to Oscar's car. Traffic was a nightmare snarl, however, and they moved at a snail's pace.

"Dude, forget this," Luis exclaimed. "I know a short cut through the city. Río, switch spots with me so I can guide him."

She got out, opened the door for him, and they swapped seats.

"Okay," indicated Luis as they began slowly moving again. "Turn onto the next street, Oscar."

After thirty minutes of weaving along dark, pitted streets, they found themselves cruising down a narrow lane called Villamain Road. Oscar was close to screaming. "Admit it, man. We're lost. You don't know where the heck we are, right?"

Luis hung his head. "Sorry, man, *me norteé*. I got turned around. But we're headed south, so, yeah, the Valley's down there somewhere."

"Fantastic," muttered Melody, slumping back against her seat. "It's already 10! I've got work tomorrow morning at 6:30."

"It gets better," Oscar said, tapping the instrument panel. "We're almost out of gas."

"I saw a gas station like five or ten minutes ago," Javier offered. "We could turn around."

Río shook her head. "No, keep going, babe. There's got to be one up ahead somewhere."

Oscar sped up, knowing he was on just fumes. They crossed a larger highway, but he kept heading south.

"Hey!" Melody shouted. "Oscar, that was 410! That loops around to 281, no?"

Luis nodded excitedly. "Yeah, man, turn around!"

Oscar slowed and turned left onto Shane Road, thinking he'd back up out again, pointing north. However, with a rattling sputter, the car stalled on the railroad tracks that ran parallel to Villamain.

"You've *got* to be kidding me," Oscar muttered. He turned the key and pumped the gas. The starter whined, but the car wouldn't start.

Javier sighed. "Told you we should've gone back to the other gas station. Now one of us is going to have to walk back, get gas in a can, and walk back. Probably two hours."

Melody smacked the back of Luis's seat. "*Menso*. Now we'll barely be arriving when I have to get ready for work. *Voy a estar toda desvelada*."

"Sleep all the way back, then, dude. You'll live."

A heated argument began about who should have to walk to the gas station. Things got a little loud, so at first they didn't quite hear the whistle blow. Río, frustrated at her friends' insults and recrimination, turned her face to the window and saw the white circle of light that was approached from the north.

"Guys?" They ignored her for a second. "Guys!" She shouted angrily. "There's a freaking train coming!"

Oscar dropped the car into neutral. "Okay, let's get out and push," he barked, jumping out of the car. As he hurried to the back of the Smurfmobile, his foot dropped into a pothole and he went sprawling. Looking up, he saw his friends beating frantically against the rear window.

Luis hopped out of the passenger seat. "Dude, your defective locks, remember?" He spun to open the door, but his sneakers slipped on the gravel that spread from the shoulder of the road to the slope of the tracks.

The train was about a hundred yards away. Its whistle blew frantically as the conductor tried to brake. Oscar and Luis regained their feet quickly, but before they could start pushing, *the car began to move on its own*.

"What the...?" As Oscar stumbled across the tracks in pursuit of his automobile, he noticed a strange shimmering light at the rear bumper. He and Luis yanked open the back doors, and the other three tumbled out, shaking with fear.

The train trundled past. Melody threw up near a mesquite on the side of the road.

"Whoa," breathed Javier. "That was...close."

As his friends stood there for a moment, watching the train with blank faces, Oscar looked down Shane Road and noticed a light.

"Be right back. You guys stay here for a bit."

He walked down to the first house, a white stucco building with a wrought-iron fence surrounding it. A man emerged at his knock, and Oscar explained the situation. The stranger agreed to help them, pulling a 5-gallon container of gas from his tool shed.

"You were lucky," the man said as they approached the car. "You ran out of gas on the one railroad crossing where everyone is safe."

Río cocked her head and narrowed her eyes as the man fiddled with the cap of the gas tank.

"What do you mean?"

"Well, in the 1930s, they say, a busload of school kids stalled in that very spot. A freight train came bearing down on them, and the driver managed to evacuate some, but twenty-six little ones were killed when the locomotive struck." Gas gurgled from the can, and a strange cold breeze made the college students shiver. "Supposedly that's why the streets around here all have the names of children: Shane, Bobbie Allen, Cindy Sue, Laura Lee. It's to remember them."

He shook out the last drop and replaced the cap. "Thing is, the spirits of those dead kids haunt this place. Or so they say. Your car isn't the first to get a little shove of assistance."

"Wait," Melody interrupted. "You're saying that little ghosts got us off the tracks? That's just...crazy."

The man looked the five of them up and down in the darkness. "Come here, all of you," he beckoned, switching on his flashlight. He walked to the back of the car and illuminated the dusty bumper of Oscar's car.

To their astonishment, there in the dust they found dozens of little handprints, smeared from the effort of pushing them to safety.

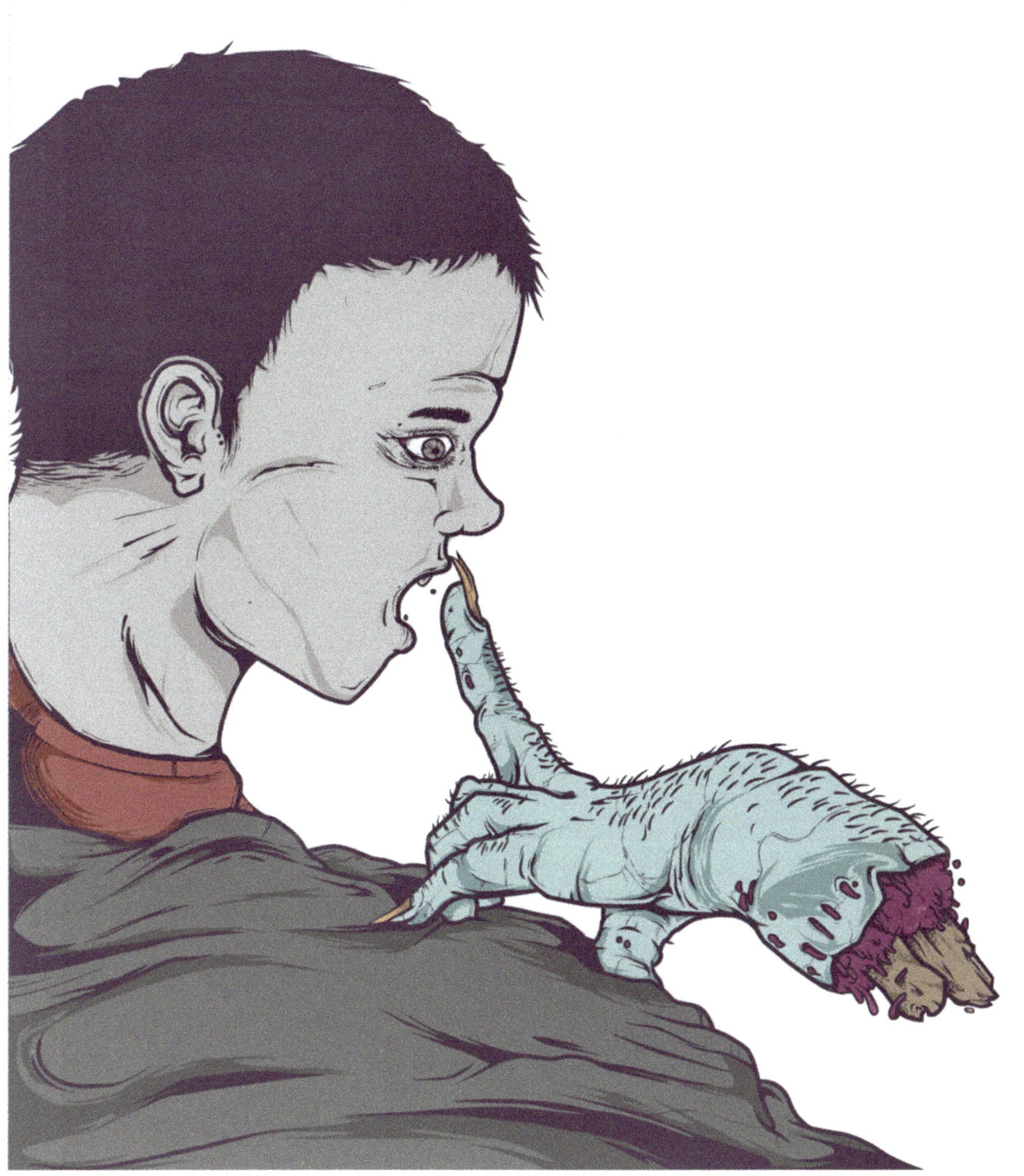

Revenge of la Mano Pachona

Ms. Peña's class was the worst group of third-graders ever. They could not be quiet, would not pay attention, refused to do their homework. They left a mess at lunch, ran amok at recess, and generally made life difficult for their teacher, a young woman fresh out of college with dreams of bettering children's lives. Fat chance. The imps in her class didn't want to change. They were completely happy with their mischievous existence.

Juanito Ortiz didn't mean to make his teacher upset. He actually liked her a lot. She was pretty and nice and smelled like lavender. But when all the other kids started cutting up, he couldn't help himself. Later he always felt guilty. He even thought about apologizing to her when no one was around.

He would one day wish he had.

After the first six weeks, something must have snapped in Ms. Peña. She came to school dressed in black, turned the lights down low, and told her students a very scary tale.

"Have you ever heard of *la mano pachona,* students?" Many of them had, they told her excitedly. Others had no idea. "*Pachona* means furry. *Mano* means hand. You see, *la mano pachona* is a hairy claw that crawls around by itself, with no body at all, doing dark deeds. My grandmother always called it the *demon hand.* No one knows for sure where the demon hand comes from, of course. Some say that a Mayan wizard was tortured by Spanish priests long ago, and just before his limbs were chopped off, he cast a spell on his right hand. He was buried in an unmarked grave so no one could find him. But the soil had not yet settled above his body when the hand crawled into the light of a full moon and began its mission of revenge."

At this point, every boy and girl in the class was absolutely still, riveted either by fear or fascination. Ms. Peña leaned closer.

"Its favorite victims," she said softly, "are bad children, disobedient little ones who act like unchained wild animals. It sneaks into their bedrooms, hides beneath their beds in or in their closets, waits for them to fall asleep..." her voice got suddenly louder "*...and curls its nasty fingers around their legs, their arms, their faces!*"

Several students squeaked in shock. Others rubbed misty eyes. Juanito's heart was beating like a hummingbird. He could imagine the demon hand, gnarled and hairy, lying in wait even now...

"So, my sweet little charges, when you get into bed today, be sure to run and jump onto the mattress, no matter what your parents say. No one wants to feel the furry touch of that black claw as it closes around your ankle and pulls you into the darkness..."

For the next week, the children were very well behaved. Most of them worried that their bad behavior would cause the demon hand to track them down. But, as is true with all kids, their fears faded with time, and old habits crept back in.

"Boys and girls," Ms. Peña warned as she tried to get them back to their seats, "remember what I told you about *la mano pachona.*"

"*N'hombre,*" grunted one particularly mean boy, Zamudio Iglesias. "*Chale*, miss. There's no *mano pachona*. You're just trying to make us shut up by scaring us."

"Are you sure of that, Mr. Iglesias?"

"*Simón*. I double-dare that stupid demon hand to come and get me. Even if he would come, I would flush him down the toilet!"

Most of the kids laughed. Not Juanito, though. He figured it was better to be safe than sorry. He didn't want *la mano pachona* to get the wrong idea about him.

The next day, Zamudio was changed. His eyes were wide, he sat bolt upright at his desk, he never joked and he always answered when the teacher called on him. At lunch, he ate all his food, even the steamed vegetables, and neatly put his tray away. The other students asked him what was wrong, but he wouldn't reply, other than to duck his head and avert his eyes.

Other kids took his place as class clown, and one by one they returned to school after Ms. Peña's warning in the same state as Zamudio. The remaining students, fearing whatever curse had clearly befallen their classmates, stopped misbehaving without any more reminders. The class was docile, obedient. Ms. Peña's smile grew wider and wider with each day.

Juanito tried desperately not to get out of line, to act exactly the way his teacher expected. But boys will be boys, and one day a student from another class pointed out a cool frog during recess. Juanito went scuttling after it, trying to catch the slick amphibian. He strayed from his group against Ms. Peña's strict instructions.

Just as he closed his hands around the slippery, mottled skin, someone yanked him back. It was his teacher. She looked very upset.

"Juanito," she scolded him, "I guess you simply want to learn the hard way, don't you?"

"No, ma'am. I...I'm s-s-sorry."

"Well, let's just hope *la mano pachona* doesn't decide to teach you a lesson. You know how it hates disobedient children."

The whole rest of the day, Juanito's palms and stomach ached as he glanced around him constantly, worried that the demon hand could be waiting for him anywhere. At home that night he dreaded bedtime, and he did everything he could to stay up later than usual. But finally his mother put her foot down, making him shower and get into bed.

Juanito lay in the dark a long time, twitching at every shadow or noise. Gradually, though, not even his fear could keep his eyelids from drooping, and sleep overtook him at last.

Shortly after midnight, he jerked awake, confused, his heart beating fast. A skittering sound came from beneath his bed. Juanito sat up, pressed his back against the headboard, pulled his pillows tightly close to him. A narrow strip of light from the hall bathroom fell across the sheets and dimly lined the deep shadows of his bedroom.

To Juanito's horror, a gruesome shape came crawling into that light, a five-legged hairy monstrosity lifting a stump-like tail into the air: it was *la mano pachona*, and it spidered its way across the bed to his folded legs, its long nails leaving strange indentations in the mattress.

"No..." whispered Juanito, this throat clenching with terror, making it impossible for him to cry out. "No, please."

The hand scrambled up his left leg, its weight and claws painful, and stood upon the pillows, just inches from the boy's face.

Juanito, trembling uncontrollably, sucked in air and fought to release a scream.

The disembodied hand lifted its index finger and waggled it back and forth. *No.*

He choked back a sob, but didn't make a sound.

Creeping closer, the hairy claw laid that index finger beside the boy's nose. Its touch was too much. He began to pass out.

La mano pachona slapped him awake. It laid that gnarled, hairy finger across his lips, then ran it sideways across his throat. Then it eased away from him and waited.

He understood after a second or two. It was waiting for an answer.

"You want me to be quiet. In class. Or you'll...you'll kill me."

The demon hand tightened into a fist, then opened its fingers quickly, springing backward onto the bed. It lifted its index finger again, flexed it twice. *Yes.*

Then it scuttled away into the darkness.

As he sat there, his heartbeat slowing as he pondered his doom, Juanito caught a whiff of a familiar smell.

Lavender. His teacher's perfume.

The Witch Owl

The silent, ghostly flight of the screech owl, along with its sinister, ghastly song, make it one of the most naturally frightening birds in the world. Those huge eyes in the middle of that round, almost human face—framed by two feathery tufts like demonic horns—complete the harrowing picture.

Ask nearly anyone in Mexico or South Texas, and they will tell you the same thing: many of the screech owls—*lechuzas*—flitting about at night are actually witches who have transformed themselves into these birds to cause trouble of one sort or another.

Tales of such creatures have been told in Mexico for more than five centuries. In Aztec lore a *chîchtli* was also a sort of shape-shifting witch that assumed the form of a screech owl, using a brand of Mesoamerican magic known as *chîchyôtl*. Modern beliefs in these beings, as a result, reflect very ancient traditions.

A witch owl, the old folks say, can appear at any time and any place. However, they seem to prefer lonely streets and highways, late at night, where they target bleary-eyed drivers and passengers in passing cars. They also apparently enjoy tapping at the window of children and teens and then staring at the youngsters for as much as an hour before either flying away—a good sign—or opening their beaks to let loose a spine-tingling cry—clearly a very evil omen.

People who are frightened by the appearance of a witch owl can try one of four basic remedies to get rid of it: prayer, tying seven knots in a string or rope, hiring a *curandera* or shooting the bird with a shotgun.

That is, unless the witch owl attacks first.

When Samuel Garza moved to Weslaco in the summer of 1984, he pretty quickly fell in with the wrong crowd. Down the street from him lived a pair of mischievous identical twins, Andrés and Estéban, who together with their cousin Rolando induced the new kid on the block to break all sorts of rules. They would sneak out late at night and shoot street lights out with their BB guns. At school they stole biology specimens, drained the formaldehyde, and dropped the dead snakes and frogs in the most awkward of places. They played pranks on anyone they found annoying, from nerds to jocks.

Now, Samuel had not been raised to be a hooligan. In fact, his father was a layman at the local parish, and his grandmother had done all she could to instill in him not only good Catholic principles, but also a real fear of the supernatural consequences of bad behavior. There was a part of him that recoiled from the mayhem he was causing, but the joy of friendship kept him from listening to his conscience.

Things came to a head, however, when he decided to pick on Barry Bustamonte, a chubby freshman who lived across the street.

"Hey," Samuel jeered one day, "so did your mom bare her bust in the *monte*, dude? Is that how you got your name?"

"Shut up! Stop making fun of me, Samuel, or I swear I'll tell my aunt."

The twins and Rolando erupted into laughter. "Careful, Sammy! His aunt's going to come around and kick your teeth in, dude!"

Barry ran off, crying. Those tears made harassing him even more enticing, however. The little gang of miscreants tagged the walls of the high school with all sorts of cruel, crude wordplay involving Barry's last name and his weight. Soon the entire freshman class had singled out the boy as a target.

One day, Barry didn't come to school. His tormentors got called into the office, but they remained close-lipped about the bullying, admitting to nothing. Such had they pacted earlier in the year.

That night, however, sleep did not come easy to Samuel. He tossed and turned in his bed for the better part of an hour, fighting off pangs of conscience and strange butterflies in the stomach. It seemed he had only just dropped into fitful slumber when a noise outside his window jerked him to wakefulness.

There, on a thick branch of the mesquite tree in his back yard, sat the biggest screech owl Samuel had ever seen. White as bleached bones in the moonlight, it glared at him with palpable hatred and rage.

Remembering the stories his grandmother had told him as a boy, he gasped through suddenly parched lips.

"*Lechuza.*"

The spectral bird spread its vast wings and opened a beak the black of ancient obsidian. The guttural cry that emerged from its plumed chest rent the night and sent chills of terror and panic along Samuel's spine.

Then the witch owl erupted from its perch and burst through the window, sending shards and splinters in every direction as it dove toward the bed. Claws the length of his forearm wrapped around Samuel, and the feathered monster ripped the teen from his room, wheeling off into the night.

Overcome by despair as the predator mounted higher and higher, Samuel lost consciousness.

When he came to some indeterminate time later, he found himself lying amid bones that glinted starkly beneath the stars. He saw the skulls then, sockets full of black night and oblivion. They were human.

"You should have left my nephew alone," creaked an unnatural voice above him. "He is a good boy and did not deserve your torture."

Samuel looked up into the now impassive face of the witch owl. It cocked its head at an impossible angle. "On the other hand," it said, "I am very hungry."

La Llorona by the Canal

Since Sylvia was very little, her mother had told her the tale. Many years ago, she always began, when this town was first founded, a beautiful young woman fell in love with a wealthy man. Though his family tried to stop the man from marrying someone with no riches or land, the two were soon happily wed. Cut off from money and power, however, the husband came to resent all the hard work he had to do. A child was born, then a second, and the marriage soured under the economic strain. When the opportunity came for the man to regain his wealth by leaving his wife and children, he did not hesitate.

The woman, finding herself abandoned with two fatherless daughters, went mad with sorrow and rage. Walking the girls down to the nearby canal in the predawn dark, she leapt into the water with them, holding their heads down till they struggled no more, then surrendering herself to the deep, silty flow.

Now, Sylvia's mother would always add, her spirit haunts the canals and reservoirs of our town, searching for her little ones. If she catches you there at the water's edge, she might mistake you for own of her own and drag you down into the depths with her.

Ah, but Sylvia's mother, like la Llorona herself, was dead now. Sylvia whispered the old stories to her little sister Greta late at night, but it just wasn't the same. Greta would whimper, calling softly for their mother. But an accident had claimed her life nearly a year ago, and the girls were left grieving with a father who, because of the demands of his job, had little time to ease their sorrow.

One evening, however, Greta's normally somber face was lit up by a smile. "I seen mamá," the five-year-old said. "In the window. She is so pretty, Sylvia."

Sylvia looked at the wedding photo hanging in the living room. Her mother's light brown eyes stared down at her with compassion. "She was beautiful, Greta. But she's gone. We can't see her anymore."

"But I did!" Greta insisted. "She told me come outside. We can go outside, Sylvia? See mamá?"

Though just three years older than her sister, Sylvia felt suddenly the impatience of a typical adult, coupled with her own longing. "Quit being silly, Greta. Mamá is dead. We're never going to see her again, okay? So just stop it."

Her lip trembling with shocked sadness, Greta rushed to their bedroom and slammed the door. Sylvia immediately felt guilty, but she figured it was for the best. They both needed to get used to the idea of life with no mother. It was useless to wish things were different. Fantasy, their father always said, is dangerous. In real life you face facts and deal with them, or you pay a hefty price.

Sylvia sat down to watch some TV. Her father, who had been working outside on the semi he drove for a living, poked his head inside.

"M'ija, where's Greta?"

"In the bedroom."

"Okay. *Mira*, I need to run to the auto parts store before they close to pick up a few things. You'll be alright?"

"Yes, *papi*. Just watching my show."

"Good. Ahorita regreso."

Sylvia sighed when she realized a re-run was on. Feeling a little guilty about being so hard on Greta, she headed to the bedroom.

It was empty. The window was open.

"Greta?" Sylvia rushed to the curtains, stuck her head outside. "Greta!"

Slipping on her sneakers, Sylvia rushed outside and glanced all around. The moon was full, and there in the distance she could make out a little figure, heading in the direction of the main irrigation canal.

"Greta!" she screamed, breaking into a run. "Stop! Stop right now!"

She ran for what seemed like forever, her lungs burning, her muscles aching. *Stay away from the canal*, her mother had told them again and again. *Or la Llorona will get you.*

Finally, just a few meters from the water's edge, Sylvia caught up to her sister. Panting, she grabbed Greta by the shoulders.

"Are...you...crazy? You can't come here in the dark, stupid! It's dangerous."

"But, Sylvia," her little sister muttered, tears welling in her eyes, "look! It's her!"

Sylvia lifted her gaze to follow Greta's finger. There, floating above the water, was the most beautiful woman she had ever seen: long, flowing tresses, honey-gold eyes, a lovely white gown that shimmered in the moonlight. For an instant, Sylvia's longing transformed the apparition, layering it with the familiar features of her own mother.

"Mamá?" she whispered, taking a step toward the lip of the canal.

"Told you," Greta said with a giggle, surging forward. "It's her. She came back for us!"

But at that moment the enchantment fell away. The figure leaned toward Greta, arms outstretched, and suddenly became a horrific figure, hair spidering wildly in all directions, nails long and cruel, face contorted in a rictus of death.

"¡MIS HIJAS!" cried the Llorona with her damned, spectral voice. "¿DÓNDE ESTÁN MIS HIJAS?"

Terrified, Sylvia reached for her sister just as the spirit's hands swept down toward them. She felt herself drawn into that cold, ghostly embrace, saw herself teeter with Greta just inches from the inky water and certain death.

"NO!" The shout came from all around them. The frigid claws of la Llorona released them, and Sylvia saw the ghost struggling in the grip of another spectral form, one whose face she knew and loved so well that it filled her dreams every night.

"Mamá!"

"Go!" their mother called. "Go my sweet ones and live your lives. I am watching over you. And I will always love you!"

And with the sound of muffled wails and silver bells, she dragged la Llorona away into the stars.

Dancing with a Ghost

A week before prom, Bobby Mendoza's girlfriend broke up with him. They had been going steady since Kennedy's election, but Mary Handy said things were getting too serious. She needed to be alone for a while.

Of course, Bobby knew the real reason for the break-up. Ever since their school's varsity team, the Donna Redskins, had blazed its way to the state championship, Mary had been eyeing a certain burly lineman. Bobby had pretended not to notice, figuring it for a silly crush, but boy, was he ever wrong. The girl was star-struck, and there was no competing with that sort of fame. The rumor mill quickly confirmed Bobby's suspicions: his former gal would be on the athlete's arm at the prom.

Telling his parents was going to be tough. The old man was always bragging about his eastside son and how he'd caught himself a girl *de buena cuna* from across FM 493. And mamá had fairly doted on Mary when she had visited—*mi güera* this, *mi nuerita* that. She would be heartbroken. Heck, *everyone* was going to be disappointed. His brothers would ridicule him and ask why he hadn't pounded the creep for being on the make and stealing his steady.

Right. Like a tuba player is going to take on a hulking football star. No, thanks.

So Bobby kept the news to himself for the time being. He rented his tux, bought a corsage, went through the motions. It was depressing as all get out, but he figured he could make up a more interesting and less humiliating break-up story for after the dance.

Friday came at last, and Bobby's father handed him the keys to the family's '55 Dodge Suburban. "Drive safe," he said, shaking his son's hand as if they were simply two men. "Try to be home by midnight."

Swallowing heavily, Bobby nodded and walked to the station wagon. He pulled out of the driveway slowly and threaded his way through quiet streets, past East Donna Elementary and toward FM 493. He waited at the stop sign, considering his options. North toward 83 and then west to Main Street? No. He was not eager to get to the dance. The sun was slipping down the spring sky, spreading the long, lonely shadows of mesquite and acacia across the road. Wanting nothing more than to simply mope, Bobby drove south.

A rush of gloomy inspiration made him turn on South Avenue and cruise along the length of the city cemetery, running his eyes over the gravestones and nodding.

I've got more in common with those stiffs than with all the happy seniors at prom. Should've just told my folks the truth. This is stupid.

He glanced back at the road and immediately slammed both feet on the brakes. A girl stood in the street not more than a yard away. She looked at him with almost empty eyes, dark brown and beautiful. Dressed in an elegant but out-of-style dress, she seemed utterly lost.

Putting the car in park, Bobby got out and approached her. "Are you okay? Why are you standing in the middle of the road? I could've hit you."

"I'm fine," she muttered languidly. "I'm just trying to get to the dance."

"The prom? Walking?"

She gazed at him strangely. "No one picked me up."

"Not even your date?"

The girl bit her lip nervously.

She doesn't have a date, he realized. This could turn a bummer of a night into a really choice experience.

He tried to be casually debonair. "Well, if you want a lift, I'm headed to the prom myself."

She nodded, her dark ponytail bouncing off her delicate shoulders. "That would be keen."

Bobby opened the door for her and then got behind the wheel again. As he began driving, he asked, "You don't go to Donna High School, do you? I've never seen you around."

Smoothing her dress several times, the girl responded, "I'm from Donna, but I've been...away for about a decade or so."

"Welcome back to the Reservation," he said with a smile. "My name's Roberto Mendoza. Everyone calls me Bobby."

"I'm Julia. Julia Ávila."

The dance floor was thick with couples when Bobby walked in with Julia on his arm, his corsage around her wrist. The live band had just finished a set, and a teacher doing DJ duty put a record on to fill the silence. It was The Marcels' doo-wop version of "Blue Moon," and Julia immediately tugged at his jacket in excitement.

"I love this song!" she exclaimed. "I mean, it's different from the way Mel Tormé sings it, but it's awful keen. Let's dance, Bobby!"

Though he didn't need any more motivation than her eager dark eyes, Bobby noticed Mary Handy staring at him from beside her dumb Adonis, who apparently didn't want to take her for a twirl. Smiling, Bobby guided his own date to the crowd that swirled under twinkling lights. Though Julia didn't seem to know any of the newest dance crazes, he soon adapted to her old-fashioned style, and they were applauded appreciatively several times by other seniors.

Finally, the soothing strains of Bert Kaempfert's "Wonderland by Night" began to sound, and Julia leaned into Bobby for the slow almost waltzing rhythms. She smelled faintly of lilies and marigolds, and though superficially cold, her skin glowed with an earnest inner heat. He began to believe he could get over Mary Handy. Let the stupid jock have her. The otherworldly beauty and grace of Julia easily outshone her.

Julia noticed his occasional glances, of course. "Who is that?" she asked.

His face red, Bobby apologized. "I should be ignoring her, sorry. That's the girl I was going steady with until about a week ago. And next to her is the oaf she left me for."

"She's a fool," Julia said. "Nice guys like you are hard to find. They only come around once in a blue moon."

Bobby felt on top of the world for the next hour or so. But the evening gradually wound down, and one by one the couples abandoned prom. Bobby escorted his date back to the car, draping his jacket across her shoulders when he saw her shiver from the cool night air. Then he reluctantly drove her back to South Avenue.

"Which house is yours?" he asked as they neared the spot where he'd almost hit her.

She looked with squinted, almost confused eyes for a moment, then pointed at a green home with white trim about a block away. "That's it. But drop me off here, Bobby. I don't want a lot of questions and hassle."

"Okay, I understand. I just have to know...Can I see you again? We have something, I think you'll agree. Chemistry. Something."

Julia looked at him for a long time before leaning across the seat to kiss him. When she pulled away, there were tears in her eyes, but she was also smiling. "Sure, Bobby. Once in a blue moon," she whispered cryptically. Then she slipped from the car and disappeared into the dark spaces beneath the trees.

It wasn't until he got home that he realized she had his suit coat with her.

I'll get it in the morning, he thought. Great excuse to see her again and maybe meet her folks.

In his dreams loomed her dark hair and eyes, the creamy coffee of her skin, the marigold smell that clung to her lightly. She seemed to twist in the air around him, floating in and out of focus. The only constant was her voice, singing softly:

Blue moon—
You saw me standing alone
Without a dream in my heart
Without a love of my own.

The sunlight slatting through his window awakened Bobby, and he quickly had breakfast and got the keys from his dad. He was soon pulling into the driveway of the little green house. A gray-haired woman came to the door when he knocked.

"Buenos días," he said, ducking his head respectfully. "*Soy Roberto Mendoza*. Is Julia up? I need to ask her for something."

"*Pero, ¿cómo dices?* Ask her? My boy, Julia is dead." A pained look of sorrow slackened the woman's face.

Bobby's heart lurched. "Dead? How? When? I just saw her last night!"

The woman's eyes narrowed in warning. "*Conque esto sea una broma, te juro que...* Listen. Julia's been dead for 12 years, Roberto."

"But...but that's impossible, ma'am! I dropped her off just before midnight, just a block up the road. I even leant her my suit coat."

"Well, you might not be playing a joke on me, but someone must be pranking you, boy. Trust me, I know when my daughter died. Twelve years ago, almost exactly. She waited for Jesse Palancares for an hour before heading to the prom by herself. She was probably so distracted by her boyfriend's betrayal that she didn't even hear the car careening down the street. *Ay, Diosito santo.* They say she died immediately. No suffering."

Bobby rubbed his eyes and tried to understand. His head was pounding, and he felt short of breath. Mrs. Ávila, seeing his confusion, stepped onto the porch and took him by the hand.

"*Vente.* It's easier if I just show you."

She led him across the street to the city cemetery. They wended among the withering flowers till the old woman jerked to a stop, her breath catching in surprise.

"Ah, Virgencita. Cuídamela siempre."

Bobby stepped forward. It was a small headstone, inscribed simply:

Julia Ávila
1922-1949
Hija Amada

Draped across the grave among lilies and marigolds was Bobby's jacket. He stooped to pick it up, and a small square of paper fluttered from its folds. Snatching it out of the air with trembling hands, Bobby read Julia's message for him:

Dearest Bobby, remember that you're a nice guy, one of a kind. Be happy. And if you ever need to dance, remember our song.

"Oh, sweet Mother of God," Mrs. Ávila whispered, tears welling in her rheumy eyes as she stared at the note. "That's her handwriting. *¡Es la letra de mi hija!*"

Overcome with awe and grief, Bobby plucked a marigold from the girl's tomb and pressed it to his heart.

And so the story ends. Bobby Mendoza went on to college, got married, settled down in his hometown and lived a normal, mostly happy life.

There are those who claim, however, that every two or three years, when some month has boasted a second full moon—a *blue* moon, as we call them—you can find him standing in that cemetery, waiting for the smell of marigolds.

Waiting to dance.

Los Duendes

"Time for bed," announced Mrs. Castro. "Get your PJs on, Julian, and brush your teeth."

"Okay, mommy."

Julian Castro had experienced a bit of a growth spurt before his fifth birthday, so he could reach the sink without a step. After rebuttoning his pajama shirt, he set his teddy bear on the toilet seat and made careful swirls across his teeth with the toothbrush. He always tried to be a good boy, though his parents didn't seem to notice much. They had their jobs and their friends. Julian was expected to keep out of the way and let them live their lives, so he made himself as invisible as possible.

Clicking off his bedroom light, he rushed to the bed, clutching Teddy tightly. His parents refused to get him a nightlight, so he left the door ajar a bit so some weak illumination would filter in.

He prayed that tonight he wouldn't hear the sounds. Laughter from the living room comforted him somewhat, though it had nothing to do with him. At the very least, it was loud enough to drown out any noise from the walls.

In the middle of the night, though, when the house was still, Julian jerked awake with a start. For a moment he lay still, listening to the frightened flutter of his own pulse. Then the scratching began, soft but persistent, first from the vicinity of his closet, then spreading through all four walls of his room.

After a while the whispering started, too. Julian couldn't quite make out the frightening words, but there were dozens of different voices all around him, even in the ceiling and, he realized with a whimper, under his bed.

From time to time they seemed to rasp his name.

In the morning, bleary eyed and terrified, Julian fumbled to get ready for daycare. His mom chatted on her cell phone the whole way, then patted his head before he stumbled out of the car. By naptime he was ready to collapse, and he slept through the entire afternoon.

At the dinner table that evening, his father looked at him unhappily. "Julian, your daycare teachers tell us that you have been taking ridiculously long naps this week. *¿Qué te pasa?* Are you getting up when we're asleep and watching TV or something? You know that's against the rules."

"No, Daddy. I'm just..." He took a deep breath. "I can't sleep."

"*Tonterías*," his mother said. "Of course you can sleep. You just don't want to. You're trying to ruin things for me." She turned to Mr. Castro. "Do something with the kid. I don't have time for this."

His father gave him a stern lecture and threatened punishment. Julian kept quiet. Just before bedtime, he drank a glass of milk and sneaked a sip of the medicine that always made him drowsy. *Not tonight,* he thought as he pulled the covers up around Teddy and himself. *No whispers tonight.*

But the scratching and voices returned that night and every other night for weeks.

"It's *los duendes*," his friend Roberto told him at daycare. "Little monsters that live in the walls and steal kids."

Terrified of being stolen while dreaming, Julian snatched what sleep he could after school. As long as sunlight poured in through the windows, his walls were silent. But once twilight deepened across his neighborhood, the skittering sounds began afresh.

His daycare called his father again, concerned. Julian broke down when his parents confronted him.

"There's something in the walls," he moaned softly between sniffles. "Scratching. Whispers. I can't sleep! *Son duendes*."

"Oh, great," his mother sighed. "The kid's going nuts. We can't afford a freaking psychiatrist!"

"Now Julian," his father said, unbuckling his belt, "that's enough of this foolishness. Do you want a spanking?"

"No, Daddy. Please. I'm sorry."

That night he stole cotton balls from his mother's make-up desk and stuffed them in his ears. Then he put his pillow over his head, hugging Teddy close. Sleep came, uninterrupted and lovely. There were no dreams.

In the morning, however, he was awakened by his mother's angry shouts.

"Julián Javier Castro! Get your little butt in here!"

He hurried into the living room, where his mother was standing over a lamp that lay broken on the tile. “Why did you do this?”

“I didn’t, Mommy?”

“Well, I sure as heck didn’t, *huerco chiflado.* Your father didn’t either. There’s no one else but you.”

Julian ducked his head. “Maybe it was...*los duendes.*”

She grabbed his pajama top and pulled him closer. “You’re not fooling anybody with that nonsense. You’re sneaking in here late at night. I know you are.”

“¿Amor?” Julian’s father called. “Have you been in the kitchen? It’s a mess! Pots and pans everywhere.”

Mrs. Castro’s face twisted in anger. “That’s it. Tonight I’m locking you in.”

Julian spent the entire day dreading the night. His parents sent him to bed right after dinner, and true to her word, his mother had Mr. Castro switch the doorknob around so they could lock it from the outside.

There was no chance of grabbing cotton balls. There was no protection. Julian lay in the gloaming and waited, trembling.

The scratching came, fiercer than ever before. The whispers got louder and louder. Finally he could hear them speaking to him.

“Julian, come with us. Leave your vile, selfish parents. We love you. They don’t. Why fight? Why stay? You’ll have such fun in *Centlani,* the Goblin Realm.”

The shadows of his room seemed to roil and writhe, and then they appeared. Green-skinned, red-eyed, each unique, some with suckered tentacles, others with clicking claws. About his height, the grotesque creatures crept closer and closer to his bed.

“*Los duendes,*” Julian whispered.

“Yes,” one of them snarled, pulling back the covers. “Goblins. *Centlapachtônhuân.* And we’re here to take you away, to make you one of us, Julian. We like you. We need you.”

Their creepy kindness surprised the boy, touched his heart. When they seized him, he did not struggle. It was for the best. His parents would have some peace at last.

“Okay,” he breathed. “But can I take Teddy with me?”

The goblins nodded, giggling hideously as their tentacles pulled him into the shadows.

El Cucu

When his parents dropped him off at his grandmother's house for a week-long visit, Roman Álvarez figured he would have even more freedom than his hands-off parents already gave him. She had spoiled him last summer, after all, cooking all his favorite foods and taking him everywhere he wanted to go. So that first night he parked himself on her ratty old couch and pulled his hoard of snacks from his backpack, ready for the wrestling marathon on his favorite cable channel.

The last match ended, but Roman's sugar rush soon had him surfing channels for wild, frenetic cartoons. Without warning, however, his grandmother switched the TV off.

"Time for bed, little one," she said.

The six-year-old groaned and kicked his feet a little against the floor. "Mom and Dad always let me stay up late," he whined. "I want to watch another show!"

His grandmother sat down on the couch next to him. "Your parents are foolish, then. Every grandmother knows that little boys and girls simply must go to bed as early as possible. Do you know why?"

"No. There's no reason. It's just dumb."

She smiled sadly and tousled his hair a bit.

"When you were smaller, I used to sing you a lullaby...Do you remember it?"

Roman shook his head, scowling and pouting. His grandmother pulled him close and shut her eyes. Then she began to softly croon.

"*Duérmete* mi niño, duérmeteme ya, porque viene el cucu y te comerá. Y si no te come, él te llevará hasta su casita que en el monte está."

Roman wanted to be tough and show the old lady that her stupid song couldn't scare him, but he felt a chill run down his spine, and he shivered against his own will.

"I thought it was called *cucuy*," he muttered, trying to sound casual despite his fluttering heart.

"It has many names, Romancito. Cuco, cucu, cucuy, coco... stuttering sounds from the mouths of a very few fearful children who have seen it in the shadows and lived, for a time, to tell the tale. All of them described the same unspeakable creature: a *Shape*, emerging from the darkness, formless, faceless and ever so cruel. Hungry to gobble up little ones still awake in the still of the night. Only sleep keeps it away, Roman, a shield of dreams that it can never shatter."

It was true that several times, when he had stayed up past midnight, his parents snoring lightly in the room next to his, Roman had sensed something in the deep shadows near his closet. But Mom and Dad wanted him to be a big boy, and they had told him that all the children's stories—Santa Claus, the Tooth Fairy, the Boogeyman—were lies. There was nothing supernatural in the world, no monsters in the darkness. So he had ignored the sensation again and again.

Nothing had ever happened. Nothing ever would.

"All right," he said, pulling away from his grandmother's embrace. "I'll go to bed, *abuela*."

She walked him to the guest bedroom where he always slept when his parents left him at her home. Tucking him tightly in, she kissed his forehead.

"*Te quiero, mi tesoro*. Sleep well. Dream wonderful dreams. Be safe."

When she shut the door, however, he flung back the covers, tiptoed to his bag, and pulled out his tablet and earbuds. Jumping back in bed, he pulled the covers over his head, turned his back toward the door, and began watching video clips, stifling a laugh or two with his pillow, popping candy into his mouth every few minutes.

Hours passed. The old house grew still. Nature itself fell silent outside. The battery of Roman's tablet died, and he yanked the covers away from his face. After the bright glow of that little screen, the darkness of the room was impenetrable. He lay there for several moments, trying to make out the objects in the room. But there were only layers upon layers of dark grey and black, indistinguishable from one another.

Porque viene el cucu... His grandmother's shaky, raspy voice echoed in his head, and the inky corners of the room become suddenly ominous.

That's stupid, he thought. There's nothing in here. Just me and the furniture.

Still, he peered breathlessly into the pitch black, straining to see the bulk of familiar things. Bed. Table. Dresser. Chair. All where he expected them to be.

And a fifth thing beside the closet, coalescing out of shadows. It moved toward him, swirling like swaths of black fabric. Step. By. Step.

Roman opened his mouth to cry out for his grandmother, but he found his voice was gone. The Shape lumbered toward the bed, its outlines growing clearer as Roman pressed himself back against the headboard. Twisted, horrible fingers clutched convulsively at the air. A swaddling of darkness twitched and slid, frayed edges floating like the hair of a drowned man. A sort of hood obscured the features as the Shape reached the bed and began to lean closer.

Roman, his breath hoarse and ragged, his body trembling like a leaf in an autumn storm, hugged himself in unspeakable fear as the thing's face finally came into view: two round empty eyes in which sable night roiled forever and a gaping mouth that hungered for his very soul.

It was the *cucu*, come at last to claim its prize, the life of a child who defied the dark.

Roman felt the black wrappings coil about his limbs, lifting him from the bed into the spasming embrace of the boogeyman. Then its maw opened wide, impossibly wide, revealing a black void unlike anything the boy's mind was capable of imagining.

And without a sound, like the silent caress of moonlit shadows upon blackened earth, the *cucu* devoured the little boy.

The Nagual of Rio Bravo

The four-person team that made up SORT—Supernatural and Occult Researchers of Texas—finished loading up their equipment in the van at about 5 pm, and they made their way to the Donna-Río Bravo International Bridge.

"Okay, so let's go over our objective," said John Madrigal, the lead investigator and founder of SORT. "For months reports have been coming out of Río Bravo that a skinwalker or shapeshifter, what we locally call a *nagual*, has been sighted around the Casa de la Cultura, transforming into a huge wolf up on the rooftop and leaping to the street, things like that. Vero, were you able to confirm any of the reports of assaults?"

Verónica Sánchez, team technician and archivist, nodded her head from the back, where she was fiddling with a laptop. "Yup. Spoke to three different women: the mother of a girl who was killed by what the media are calling a rabid dog, a woman who was assaulted by a creature she described as '*medio lobo*,' and another who barely got away from '*un perro enorme*' by ducking into a stranger's home. We're definitely dealing with a dangerous entity."

"And that's where I come in." Arnulfo "Arnie" Sandoval stopped rubbing down his nine-millimeter and hid it in the secret compartment in the floor. As the muscle of the group, it was his job to find the best way for them to protect themselves against the dark forces they often encountered. "Silver and obsidian weaken them. Hopefully we can capture the freak with the shiny net. Only thing that kills them is beheading or a bullet dipped in white ash. So I got my survivalist buddy to make us some hollow points filled with ash and silver dust. I also brought my trusty machete."

"Awesome." John looked over at Carlos Tijerina, cameraman and driver. "Anything you want to add, bro? I know your mom is from Río Bravo."

Carlos shrugged. "Just that there's this abandoned house next to the Casa de Cultura. Maybe the dude's hanging out there during the day. You guys know the history, right?" He gestured at the land just beyond the bridge they were crossing. "All that area used to be a huge estate called la Sauteña, granted to the count of el Sauto, Antonio Vicente Uriza, by the Spanish government in 1700s. The count and his descendants were pretty cruel to the poor workers, and lots of people quietly said the family was into black magic and stuff. After the Mexican Revolution, the land was given to the people, and that's basically how the city came into existence. The hacienda of la Sauteña became the Casa de Cultura. But now people say it's a haunted or cursed place."

The team fell silent as they approached the Mexican port of entry. The politician who had hired them had assured John that the van wouldn't be inspected, but the tension was palpable. What if the right *mordida* hadn't been paid? Luckily, the light was green, and Carlos was waved through without incident. They reached the city limits, weaved through the pitted streets, and parked in front of a clinic on the square just behind the historical building where the skinwalker had been sighted.

As the sun began to set, Carlos and Vero set up the lights and cameras, trying to get full 360-degree coverage of the old hacienda. John and Arnie walked the perimeter, greeted twice by transit officers who were in the know. Surreptitiously, the local authorities had cleared a two-block radius around the square.

Confident that the police would keep civilians away, John left Arnie to set up the net while he rejoined the other two. The back doors of the van were open, revealing monitors and other technical equipment.

"Definitely high levels of glim," Vero said, referring to the spiritual energy that indicated powerful spells. She tapped the screen of her laptop, which was wirelessly connected to sensors she'd place in key areas. "Coming from the abandoned house. I think our furry friend is getting ready to go for a stroll."

"Guys, who's that?" Carlos jerked his head at a screen. An old man was ambling along the road toward the Casa de Cultura.

"Wow. What a blockade the local cops put up." John sighed. "Crap. Let me go shoo this dude away."

His boots crunching against the asphalt, John hurried over to the intruder. With his hand on the grip of his pistol, he addressed the old man in Spanish.

"Can I help you with something?"

The stranger's weathered face cracked into a friendly smile. "No, but perhaps I can help you."

"What do you mean?"

"Evidently you have come to stop the *nagual*, is that not so? I see weapons, cameras, the trap your friend yonder is preparing..."

John nodded impatiently. "Yes, yes. If you must know, we are paranormal investigators. The city hired us to capture the shapeshifter or kill it if we must. So, unless you have some high-tech weaponry hidden under your flannel shirt on in the pocket of your chinos..."

"Oh, I have something better than that, my son. I have travelled many miles, all the way from Mexico City, to face the wizard who is terrorizing this town. Tell me, how do you plan to lead the beast to your silver net?"

John said nothing. It was the weakest part of the plan, the one that put them all at risk. They needed to draw or herd it to the narrow alley between the clinic and the abandoned house. But eyewitness accounts had made it clear the *nagual* moved incredibly fast, so John had serious concerns.

"I thought as much," the old man quipped in response to the silence. "Listen. I will be the bait. When he catches my scent, he will most certainly want to follow."

Before John could respond, Vero's voice came through his earpiece. "John, Arnie, you guys need to get ready. Glim is spiking like mad. Any moment now."

The old man's eyes flashed yellow. He lifted his head and scented the air.

"He comes."

"What? How do you..."

Stripping off his shirt, the stranger smiled again. "Because I am a *nagual*, too."

John backed away as the old man began to quiver and snarl, kicking away his shoes and stepping out of his pants. With a glowing ripple of blue glim, he transformed, dropping to all fours and shaking out a pelt of black-spotted gold.

"John?" Arnie's voice sounded in his ear. "You okay?"

"Uh, there is an enormous jaguar crouched here in front of me. The old man. He's a skinwalker, too. Says he can help us. I mean, he said he could. Can't say anything now."

The huge feline cocked its head at him and darted off toward the abandoned house.

"Okay, everybody," John shouted, following it. "Whether we want to or not, we've got us a four-legged partner."

"Got him!" shouted Carlos. "Rooftop. He... Dang, he kind of looks like the Wolfman or something."

Arnie chuckled incongruously. "Yeah, he froze himself mid-shift. Only the real expert ones can do that. Got us a high-ranking evil wizard, *cuates. Perrón.*"

The wolfman leapt high into the air and landed nimbly on the cracked concrete. John and Arnie rushed toward it, weapons drawn, hoping it would turn tail and head toward the trap. No such luck. The beast instead rushed toward them, snarling.

Then the jaguar slammed into it, rolling away and leaping up onto a bit of rubble from recent street improvements. The wolfman regained his feet and howled in rage, spinning to confront its attacker. The jaguar flattened itself against the rubble, readying itself, then it bounded away toward the alley.

In a single, fluid motion, the other nagual shifted completely, and in full lupine form raced after the cat. Seconds later an outraged series of barking shouts split the air.

John and Arnie hurried around the corner and found the old man, naked and human, standing over the wolf, ensnared in the silver netting. Arnie approached cautiously, pistol trained on their prisoner.

"Good job, sir," he muttered appreciatively in English.

The old man smiled. "Thank you," he replied in the same language. "Bullets? What it's in you bullets?"

"Silver. Ash."

"Ah. You smart guy." Without warning, the old man reached out and snatched the pistol away from Arnie, emptying an entire clip into the wolf. As the two paranormal investigators stared, mouths agape, the nagual reverted to human form: a young man with gang tattoos covering his entire face and torso.

"Maras," spat the old man, handing back the gun. "More worse than wizards. Or wolves. Attacking women? Naguales no do that stuff. Maras, yes."

He spat on the corpse and walked away into the darkness.

John and the rest of the SORT team spent most of the night trying to explain to the chief of police why they had a dead Guatemalan gang-banger in their net.

The Boyfriend's Death

Juan Garza and Bárbara de los Ángeles had finally, after four years of going out, decided to tie the knot. Johnny had taken longer to commit—Barbie would have married him while they were attending Donna High School, if he had asked her. Now they had graduated and Johnny was working at the Haggar's plant in Weslaco; his new stability had given him no more excuse, and he had popped the question.

Plans had been made, invitations sent out, and Saturday, January 21, 1978, the couple was set to be joined in holy matrimony at the San Juan Shrine. So when Juan's uncle asked him whether he'd gotten the marriage license yet, Juan could have slapped himself.

"Barbie," he told his fiancée, "come with me to the courthouse, yeah? I forgot the license."

"Johnny!" Barbie sighed in frustration. "Why do you always have to leave stuff till the last minute?"

"*No me estés fregando*, Barb. Just cool it. I forgot it, but it ain't too late. Let's just drive to Edinburg and get the thing, *¿sí?*"

Swallowing her irritation, Barbie nodded, and the two got in Juan's Buick and headed north on FM 493. Juan's license plate was expired, so he wanted to avoid the main highway. *Better to take 107 to Edinburg*, he thought to himself.

The farm road was sparsely populated, and very few cars drove along it between La Blanca and Donna. A cold wind was blowing from the North, and as Juan reached out his hand to switch on the heater, he noticed that he was almost out of gas.

"Crap."

"What?" Barbie asked, staring out her window at the cotton fields and grapefruit orchards. As if in response, the car started sputtering.

"We're out of gas," Johnny replied with a smirk. He pulled the Buick onto a gravel drive that led to an iron gate, the entrance to a large orange orchard.

"Great, just great. There's no gas station around here!"

"Barbie, calm down. I'm just gonna take the gas can and jog back down to the filling station on 83."

"That's like four miles back! What am I supposed to do in the meantime?"

"Just sit here, Barbie. Listen to the radio or something. Jesus, you always gotta make a big deal out of everything."

"I'm sorry," Barbie replied, her face softening. She didn't want to make Johnny mad or give him an excuse to break off their engagement. It had been tough enough manipulating him into asking her in the first place.

Juan rubbed his hands over his hair. "It's alright, *chiquita*. Look, keep the doors locked and wait for me. Hopefully I'll get a ride. If not, it'll take me about an hour to go and come back." He leaned over to give her a kiss, and a strange thrill went through her, like a premonition.

"Be careful, baby," she whispered.

"*Pos claro.*"

Barbie watched him through her window as he grew smaller and finally disappeared to the South. Flipping on the radio, she listened to the BeeGees, the Eagles, and finally some *conjunto* tunes before pulling out the key when she realized she'd run the battery down this way. She had begun to doze off when a crunching on the gravel brought her fully awake.

Standing in front of the car was a tall, dark and bearded man who held a large canvas bag in front of him. Her heart began pounding as he walked to the driver's side door and grabbed the handle. It was locked, but he yanked very hard on the door several times, each jolt sending a wave of nausea through Barbie's guts.

Finally, he leaned his face close to the window and muttered in a hoarse whisper, "*Ábreme.*"

Barbie, unable to speak, just shook her head. There was no way she was going to open the door to this weirdo. She noticed that there were thin scars all over his face, as if he'd been sliced up by a thin blade. *Or shrapnel? Maybe he's a vet?*

"*¡Dije que abras la maldita puerta!*" he shouted gruffly, and Barbie gave a stifled cry, shaking her head and sinking back against her own door. The bearded stranger took a few steps back, pulled his arm back, and swung the bag against the windshield with a shuddering thud. From the vibrations of the impact, there was apparently something heavy and hard inside. Again he swung with all his might, again and again, each blow accompanied by a muffled shriek from Barbie. Whimpering, she muttered Johnny's name over and over. Some fine cracks appeared in the glass, but it seemed unlikely that the madman could break through. Finally he seemed to get tired and dropped the bag, staring blankly at Barbie for a few minutes and then walking off into the fields across the road.

Barbie, trembling with fear, kept waiting for Juan to arrive. He would come rescue her, take her home. Then tomorrow they'd go get the license, and on Saturday they'd marry. All she had to do was wait a little longer. Eventually she turned on the radio again and realized that two hours had gone by. Carefully watching the fields for signs of the bearded attacker's return, she opened the car door. The chill wind bit into her—the sun was beginning to go down, and even in South Texas winter nights can be unmercifully cold. Slowly, her eyes scanning the darkening horizon, Barbie walked around the front of the car to the driver's side, where the canvas bag lay abandoned in the dirt. Overcome by curiosity, she knelt beside it and loosened the hemp rope that closed its mouth.

With a scream she fell back onto the gravel, cutting her hands as she kicked and dragged herself away from what now sat exposed to the twilight air—Juan's decapitated head, still recognizable despite having been slammed over and over against the windshield.

Her back against the cold metal of the gate, Barbie began to sob. Darkness was falling, her fiancé was dead, her home was miles to the south, and somewhere out there a killer was waiting...

The twilight glittered momentarily against something. Barbie looked down at the silver pendant that hung from a thin chain around her neck. The Virgin Mary. The serene smile on the figure's face evoked something from depths of her soul. Barbie twitched her head, trying to remember. *What were those words? Grandmother died when mom was little, but she told her something. What was it?*

She shuddered with epiphany as it came to her. *Somos diosas.* Goddesses. She wasn't sure what her grandmother had meant by that phrase, but it suddenly gave her the will to stand. Gripping the pendant with her bloody left hand, Barbie stood with slow deliberation, her tears drying painfully in the brisk wind. Stepping carefully around Juan's head, she walked to the trunk of the car and used the keys to open it. She grabbed the tire iron and a flashlight, and then slammed the trunk shut. Hefting the cold metal shaft, she felt strangely calm. Despite all that had happened to her–maybe even because of this tragic day—she was ready to face her destiny on her own terms.

"I'm going home now," she said out loud, perhaps to no one, perhaps to the universe. "I'm tired of being afraid. I'm not going to wait around anymore for someone to save me. My mother and father and aunts and sisters are waiting for me, just up ahead. It isn't too far, not really. So I'm going to walk down this dark road by myself, and God help anyone who tries to stop me."

Then she clicked on the flashlight and strode into the gloaming.

The Curse of the Black Witch Moth

When Carolina Escalante opened the back door to let the dog out, a huge black moth fluttered its way inside, startling the young girl. Her mother heard Carolina's frightened squeak and stepped into the kitchen. Seeing the insect hovering indecisively, the woman crossed herself and lifted a silver crucifix to her lips.

"*M'ija*, why did you let that thing in? What were you thinking?"

Carolina's lower lip trembled. "It just flew in, *mamá*. I didn't even see it. Is it poisonous?"

"Ay, worse than that, child. It's a black witch moth. It can bring fortune or death, but you never know which, so it is best to keep the bugs out of the home."

The young girl watched the moth, as big as both her hands together, its sable body mottled with a light golden skein that seemed to her imagination the time-worn loops of ancient runes. Its thick feelers probed the air, questing, sensing.

It's deciding if we get fortune or death, she realized, and the thought sent a chill along her nerves.

"If it lands above the front door, we get fortune," her mother muttered, opening the garage door and groping for the broom. "But if it flies to the four corners of this house...."

Mrs. Escalante yanked the door shut and brandished the broom, squinting at the moth and assuming an attack stance.

"What, *mamá*? What will happen then?"

"The sick will die," her mother replied, swinging the broom through the air.

Carolina gasped. The only person sick in the house was her grandfather Fernando. Though very hardy as a young man, his health had steadily worsened as he got older, mostly because he kept ignoring his doctor's recommendations. Saddled with severe diabetes, Don Fernando should have been following a strict diet and taking his insulin. But he was a stubborn, independent man who trusted his own instincts about his physical constitution.

One evening last year, the sixty-five year old had been driving back to the Río Grande Valley from Saltillo when his body had begun to feel heavier and heavier and his vision had failed him. Though he'd slowed and tried to pull off the road, he had ended up smashing against a concrete retention wall.

In the hospital, the doctors discovered his unchecked diabetes had brought on renal failure. One of his kidneys was permanently damaged, and he had been placed on hemodialysis, making weekly visits to the clinic, a tube and a bag his constant companions. As Carolina's grandmother was herself hemiplegic from a series of embolisms and living with tía Andrea in Saltillo, it had fallen to Carolina's mother to take on the responsibility of watching over Don Fernando.

Complications had set in, and now the man was essentially bed-ridden, relying completely on the attentions of Mrs. Escalante and her three daughters. Mr. Escalante, who earned his living driving trucks between Mexico and the US, was gone for most of the week but assisted on the weekends.

"Go get your sisters!" Mrs. Escalante cried as her attempts to shoo the moth back outside continued to fail.

Carolina rushed down the hall to get Angela and Elena from their room, yanking buds from their ears to make herself heard. "Mamá needs you! It's a nasty moth that wants to kill *buelito*!"

"What?" they asked in unison, hurrying to the kitchen to see what was going on.

Carolina remained behind, opening the door to her grandfather's bedroom and peering in to see how he was. His breathing was ragged and uneven in the gloom. *Alive. Thank God.*

"Carolina?" His voice was weak but sonorous, a voice meant for singing and laughter.

"Sí, soy yo. Just checking on you."

"Qué linda. You love me, child?"

A sob squeezed her chest. "Sí, abuelo. Lo quiero mucho."

He said nothing more. A light snore let Carolina know he'd slipped into sleep. From the kitchen came her mother's frustrated shout. "That's one corner! Stop it, girls! Kill it if you have to!"

Carolina ran down the hall into the living room, which contained the northeastern corner of the house. Though they swatted at it with towels, magazines and broom, the black witch moth alighted right in the corner, moving its wings slowly for a few seconds, as if mocking their frantic attempts to stop it. Then it was off again, heading for the hallway.

"Run! Shut the bedroom doors!"

All three girls hit the hallway at the same time, smashing into and stumbling over each other while the moth glided overhead and disappeared into the girls' room. Their mother, panicking, shoved them out of the way and slammed her father's door shut, pivoting to stand in front of it like a sentinel, broom at the ready.

"Ahora sí, méndiga mariposa de la muerte, let's see you get past me!"

Carolina poked her head in the bedroom she shared with her older sisters. The moth was perched in the southwestern corner of the house, waiting. A minute passed. Five. No one spoke. Elena finally took the broom from her mother's grasp and crept into the room, ready to flatten the intruder.

"Pilar!" their grandfather gasped from behind the door. "M'ija, ¡ayúdame!"

As their mother spun and swung open the door, the sinister moth launched itself and flapped like some bat from the heart of the underworld itself. Pilar Escalante had kicked the door to close it behind her as she entered, but the moth flicked itself sideways and dove in before it clicked shut.

"NOOOOO!" came the desperate cry of their mother. Angela barged in, flipping on the light.

In the southeastern corner of the Escalante residence, the black witch moth had settled the ominous breadth of its hated wings. Pilar fell to her knees beside her father, who was gasping for breath, his hands clutching at the empty air.

In seconds, Don Fernando was gone. Carolina swore she could feel his spirit drift off into the ether, freed at last from his infirm flesh.

The moth began to move again. Drained of any will by their loss, the Escalante women watched it calmly flutter out of the room. Only Carolina found the strength to stand and follow.

She found it resting above the door.

For a time, none of them could understand why the black witch moth, after bringing death, would mock them by promising fortune.

But then the man had come, three days after Don Fernando's passing. An insurance agent, he said. In his hands was a check.

Fernando Escalante's policy yielded a lump sum payment of $80,000 after funeral expenses. Like much of life, blessing and curse were wrapped up together inextricably.

Notes

For each of the folktales and legends recounted in this volume, I have provided brief notes on my initial reception of the narrative—the informant and timeframe—as well as a general idea of the contextualization I have added in my retransmission. To aid in more scholarly collection of border lore, I have additionally classified every tale using three existing indices:

Aarne-Thompson-Uther Types of International Folktales (UTA)
Jan Harold Brunvand's Urban Legend Type Index (BRUN)
Thompson's Motif Index of Folk Literature

"The Lady in Black"

Informant and circumstances of initial reception—A teacher at Lincoln Junior High School in McAllen during the early 1980s, while I was in her class.

Literary contextualization not present in original tale—Historical context and character specifics.

Folktale type—ATU 888. The faithful wife.

Motifs—E322.2.1. Dead wife returns and asks husband to go with her to spirit world. E 279.1. The ghost haunts outside at night in woman shape. E 332.1. Ghost appears at road and stream. E 334.2.1. Ghost of murdered person haunts burial spot. E 334.2.3. Ghost of tragic lover haunts scene of tragedy.

"The Big Bird"

Informant and circumstances of initial reception—My father, shortly after the actual events described.

Literary contextualization not present in original tale—Historical context and character specifics (names, reluctance to shoot).

Folktale type—ATU 1135. Eye-remedy (man injures ogre).

Motifs—G 510. Ogre killed, maimed, or captured. G 550. Rescue from ogre.

"The Devil at Boccaccio 2000"

Informant and circumstances of initial reception—A cousin of mine during the early 1980s.

Literary contextualization not present in original tale— Character specifics and musical details.

Folktale type—ATU 779. Divine rewards and punishments.

Urban legend type—BRUN 03220. The Devil in the Dancehall.

Motifs—G 303.3.12. The devil as a well-dressed gentleman. G 303.4.5.4. The devil has goat feet. G 303.4.5.9. The devil has cock's feet. G 386. The devil punishes dancing. G 836. Taboo: disobedience.

"The Ghosts of Fort Brown"

Informant and circumstances of initial reception—A fellow college student during the early 1990s, blended with tale of ghostly reconciliation heard from my grandmother.

Literary contextualization not present in original tale—Addition of *curandera* grandmother and protagonist's ability as medium.

Folktale type—ATU 766. Forgiveness and Redemption. ATU 769. A Child Returns from the Dead.

Motifs—E 281.3. Ghost haunts particular room in house. E 323.5. Mother returns to search for dead child. E 334. Non-malevolent ghost haunts scene of former misfortune, crime, or tragedy. N 825.3.3. Help from grandmother.

"Damnation at Toluca Ranch"

Informant and circumstances of initial reception—My grandmother, during my childhood. Story retold to me repeatedly over the years by different informants.

Literary contextualization not present in original tale—Historical context.

Folktale type—ATU 756B. The devil's contract.

Motifs—M 210. Bargain with the devil. M 211. Man sells soul to the devil. E 752.2. Soul carried off by the devil. Q 272.1.1. Devil carries off rich man at death.

"The One-Eyed Woman"

Informant and circumstances of initial reception—My grandmother, who claimed to have seen apparition.

Literary contextualization not present in original tale—Character specifics, historical and cultural context.

Folktale type—ATU 327E. Abandoned Children Escape from Burning Barn. ATU 777. The Wandering Jew (variant).

Urban legend type—BRUN 03210. The Phantom Coachman (variant).

Motifs—F 512.1.1. Person with one eye in center of forehead. F 601.4.2. Extraordinary companion saves hero from death.

"The Devil's Lagoon"

Informant and circumstances of initial reception—Fellow teacher in late 1990s.

Literary contextualization not present in original tale—Character details and music.

Folktale type—ATU 760. The Unquiet Grave.

Motifs—E 155. Periodic resuscitation. E 414. Drowned person cannot rest in peace. E 275. Ghost haunts place of great accident or misfortune. E 337.3. Lovers' tragedy re-enacted.

"Chupacabras in Mission"

Informant and circumstances of collection—Local media.

Literary contextualization not present in original tale—Character and victim details.

Folktale type—ATU 300. The Dragon-Slayer.

Urban legend type—BRUN 03225. Chupacabras.

Motifs— E 251.3.3. Vampire sucks blood. G 510. Ogre killed, maimed, or captured.

"The Flying Witch of Monterrey"

Informant and circumstances of collection—Social and international media.

Literary contextualization not present in original tale—Historical context and character details.

Folktale type—ATU 1653A. Securing the Door.

Motifs—G 242.1. Witch flies through air on broomstick. G 267. Man pursued by witches. G 272.1. Steel powerful against witches. G 276. Escape from witch.

"The Virgin Mary versus Satan"

Informant and circumstances of initial reception—Aunt, in the mid-1980s.

Literary contextualization not present in original tale— None.

Folktale type—ATU 1096. The tailor and the ogre in a sewing contest.

Motifs—K47.1. Sewing contest won by deception: the long thread.

"The Headless Horseman of South Texas"

Informant and circumstances of initial reception—Father, during childhood.

Literary contextualization not present in original tale—Historical context, occult connections, character details in 1960s encounter.

Folktale type—ATU 750B. The Revived Mortem.

Motifs—E 1. Person comes to life. E 232.4. Ghost returns to slay enemies. E 261. Wandering ghost makes attack. E 422.1.1.3.1. Headless ghost rides horse.

"The Sack Man"

Informant and circumstances of initial reception—Grand-mother, during childhood.

Literary contextualization not present in original tale— Historical context.

Folktale type—ATU 327C. The Devil Carries the Hero Home in a Sack. ATU 363. The Vampire.

Motifs—G 10. Cannibalism. G 13. Spiritual exaltation from eating human flesh. G 55. People who eat child become supernatural. E 251.3.3. Vampire sucks blood.

"The Ghosts of Fort Ringgold"

Informant and circumstances of initial reception—Fellow teacher in the mid-1990s.

Literary contextualization not present in original tale— Character details

Folktale type—ATU 766. Forgiveness and Redemption. ATU 750B. The Revived Mortem.

Motifs—E 281. Ghosts haunt house. E 275. Ghost haunts place of great accident or misfortune. E 761.7.8. Life token: great wind blows.

"Alicante"

Informant and circumstances of initial reception—Uncle, at his ranch in the mid-1980s.

Literary contextualization not present in original tale—A few character details.

Folktale type—ATU 300B. The King of the Snakes.

Urban legend type—BRUN 02435. The Bosom Serpent.

Motifs—B 765.4.1. Snake attaches itself to a woman's breast and draws away her milk while she sleeps. B 765.15. Snake stands up, whistles.

"The Sea Monster of Port Isabel"

Informant and circumstances of collection—Local media.

Literary contextualization not present in original tale—Character details, encounter between protagonist and monster.

Folktale type—ATU 300. The Dragon-Slayer. ATU 555. The Fisherman and His Wife (variant).

Motifs—A 421. Sea-god. G 301. Monsters. G 308. Sea monster. G 308.1. Fight with sea (lake) monster.

"Ghost Tracks of San Antonio"

Informant and circumstances of initial reception—Fellow college student in the early 1990s.

Literary contextualization not present in original tale—All characters and reason for trip to San Antonio.

Folktale type—ATU 503. The Grateful Dead.

Urban legend type—BRUN 01011. Guardian Angels.

Motifs—E 363.1. Ghost aids living in emergency.

"Revenge of la Mano Pachona"

Informant and circumstances of initial reception—Grandmother, during childhood.

Literary contextualization not present in original tale—Modern setting, characters.

Folktale type—ATU 366. The Golden Arm.

Motifs—E 422.1.11.3. Ghost as hand or hands. E 293. Ghosts frighten people (deliberately).

"The Witch Owl"

Informant and circumstances of initial reception—Grandmother, during childhood.

Literary contextualization not present in original tale—Setting and characters changed.

Folktale type—ATU 327C. The Children with the Witch.

Motifs—G 211.4.4. Witch in form of owl. G 242. Witch flies through air. G 261. Witch steals children. G 269.10. Witch punishes person who incurs her ill will. G 269.10.1. Witch kills person as punishment. G 262.0.1. *Lamia*. Witch who eats children.

"La Llorona by the Canal"

Informant and circumstances of initial reception—Grandmother, during childhood.

Literary contextualization not present in original tale—Setting and characters changed.

Folktale type—ATU 316. The Mermaid in the Pond.

Urban legend type—BRUN 03221. La Llorona.

Motifs—S 302. Children murdered. H 1219.2. Quest assigned as punishment for murder. Q 520.1. Murderer does penance. E236.2. Return from dead to demand stolen children. E 266.1. Ghost of suicide drags people into stream. E 547. The dead wail.

"Dancing with a Ghost"

Informant and circumstances of initial reception—Father, during childhood.

Literary contextualization not present in original tale—Setting, character traits.

Folktale type—ATU 407. The Flower Girl (variant).

Urban legend type—BRUN 01000. The Vanishing Hitchhiker.

Motifs—E 332.3.3.1. The vanishing hitchhiker. E 361.2. Return from dead to give consoling message. E 631.1. Flower from grave.

"Los Duendes"

Informant and circumstances of initial reception—Grandmother, during childhood.

Literary contextualization not present in original tale—Character details.

Folktale type—ATU 503. Helpful Elves.

Motifs—F 210. Fairyland. F 311. Fairies adopt human child. F 320. Fairies carry people away to fairyland. F 451.5.2.7. Dwarfs play pranks. F 452.5.2.10. Dwarfs frighten mortals.

"El Cucu"

Informant and circumstances of initial reception—Grandmother, during childhood.

Literary contextualization not present in original tale—Character details, 21st-century technology.

Folktale type—ATU 326. The Youth Who Wanted to Learn What Fear Is.

Motifs—G 442. Child-stealing demon. G 11.15. Cannibal demon. G 360. Ogres with monstrous features. G 303.5.1.1. Devil in a black cloak. Q 225. Punishment for scoffing at religious teachings.

"The Nagual of Río Bravo"

Informant and circumstances of initial reception—One of my graduate students.

Literary contextualization not present in original tale—Paranormal investigator details.

Folktale type—ATU 1160. The ogre in the haunted castle. Beard caught fast.

Motifs—G 211.2.2. Witch in form of wolf. G 221.3. Witch has extraordinary bodily strength. G 262. Murderous witch. G 263. Witch injures, enchants or transforms. G 303.25.7.1. Devil shot with silver bullet.

"The Boyfriend's Death"

Informant and circumstances of initial reception—Fellow high school student in the late 1980s.

Literary contextualization not present in original tale—Setting, character traits, closure.

Folktale type—ATU 333. Little Red Riding Hood (variant).

Urban legend type—BRUN 01300. The Boyfriend's Death.

Motifs—S 139.2. Slain person dismembered. S139.2.1.1. Head of murdered man taken along as trophy. S139.2.2.1.6. Heads brandished to intimidate foe. W32. Bravery.

"Curse of the Black Witch Moth"

Informant and circumstances of initial reception—Wife, in the late 1990s.

Literary contextualization not present in original tale

Folktale type—ATU 736. Luck and Wealth.

Motifs—M 305. Ambiguous oracle. M341. Death prophesied. N 170. The capriciousness of luck.

Bibliography

Aarne, Antti. *The Types of the Folktale: A Classification and Bibliography*. Translated and Enlarged by Stith Thompson. 2nd revised edition. Helsinki: Suomalainen Tiedeakatemia / FF Communications, 1961.

Bennett, Gillian and Paul Smith. *Contemporary Legend: A Reader (New Perspectives in Folklore)*. New York: Routledge , 1996.

Bowles, David. *Creature Feature*. McAllen, Texas: AIM Media Texas, 2013.

———. *Mexican Bestiary*. Donna, Texas: VAO Publishing, 2012.

———. *The Seed: Stories from the River's Edge*. Spring, Texas: Absey & Co., 2011.

Brunvand, Jan Harold. *Encyclopedia of Urban Legends, Updated and Expanded Edition*. 2nd revised edition. Santa Barbara: ABC-CLIO, 2012.

Glazer, Mark. *Flour from Another Sack & Other Proverbs, Folk Beliefs, Tales, Riddles, & Recipes*. Revised edition. Edinburg, TX: Pan American University Press, 1994.

Robe, Stanley L. *Index of Mexican Folktales*. Folklore Studies 26. Berkeley: University of California Press, 1973.

Thompson, Stith. *Motif-Index of Folk-Literature: A Classification of Narrative Elements in Folktales, Ballads, Myths, Fables, Mediaeval Romances, Exempla, Fabliaux, Jest-books, and Local Legends*. Revised and enlarged edition. Bloomington: Indiana University Press, 1955-1958.

Uther, Hans-Jörg. *The Types of International Folktales: A Classification and Bibliography Based on the System of Antti Aarne and Stith Thompson*. Vols 1-3. FF Communications No. 284-86. Helsinki: Academia Scientiarum Fennica, 2004.

www.ingramcontent.com/pod-product-compliance
Lightning Source LLC
Chambersburg PA
CBHW041753010726
47507CB00009B/382

* 9 7 8 1 9 4 2 9 5 6 0 1 3 *